CURSE OF THE SANDTONGUE

BRAVELANDS

THE VENOM
SPREADS

BRAVELANDS

CURSE OF THE SANDTONGUE

BRAVELANDS

THE VENOM
SPREADS

ERIN
HUNTER

HARPER
An Imprint of HarperCollinsPublishers

Library of Congress Control Number: 2021948582
ISBN 978-0-06-296688-9

Typography by Ellice M. Lee
21 22 23 24 25   PC/LSCH   10 9 8 7 6 5 4 3 2 1
❖
First Edition

With special thanks to Rosie Best

PROLOGUE

The sun sparkled on the surface of the watering hole as Gorge the crocodile gently let the top of her head break through the water. She opened her eyes just a fraction. Perfectly hidden, the ridged brown skin of her forehead camouflaged among reeds and broken twigs, she splayed her legs and floated, gazing at the bank where a zebra herd had gathered to drink. The world above the water was hot and bright, and even through the water she could hear the thumping of the zebra herd's hooves as they drank.

It wasn't hard to choose her prey. A zebra foal, drinking deeply, some way from the rest of the herd. As she watched, it flicked its ears, which were still too big for its head, and one of its clumsy hooves slipped a little on the sandy bank.

A quiet croak of satisfaction escaped Gorge's throat as a stream of tiny bubbles. These grasstongues who ran in big, noisy herds never taught their young to survive the way they should. The foal would be an easy target for hungry crocodiles, and the herd would run at the first sign of trouble, abandoning one to save the rest.

She glanced from side to side, trying to pick out any competition. But she couldn't see a single one of her bask, neither the bumps of their foreheads above the water nor the telltale dark shapes moving beneath it. She felt no stirring currents along her flanks.

She narrowed her eyes.

Surely she couldn't be the only one to have spotted this easy meal?

She sank down under the water and used her tail to glide toward the spot on the bank, peering around through the silt and reeds as she went. Perhaps Feast or Writhe was hiding down there, biding their time, and planning to ambush any other crocodiles who came near. It wouldn't be unusual for a fight to break out between them over a juicy morsel like this. Gorge had won and lost plenty of them in her time, and she had the scars to prove it.

But there was still no sign of the bask, even as the water grew shallower and the ripples from the foal's lapping tongue passed over Gorge's head. She floated to a stop, holding tense and still, until she saw the shadow of a muzzle descend and touch the surface.

Then with a powerful thrust and a thrash of her tail, Gorge reared out of the water, her jaws wide.

She saw it all, in a bright flash—the endless blue sky above, the rolling, terrified eye of the young zebra, the panicking and prancing of its kin, the mud kicking up under their hooves as they scrambled away.

The foal's legs shuddered and slipped in the muddy bank, too frightened to stay still, too shocked to get away.

Gorge's jaws closed over its haunch. She heard the scream and tasted blood, then simply let the weight of her muscular body drag her and her prey back and down, into the water. The zebra flailed as she pulled it under, bleating and thrashing, sending up a curtain of bubbles and churning silt.

Gorge simply waited. She had learned from her own mother, as all crocodiles did, that this was the grasstongue's final trick. Clever crocodiles wouldn't fall for it—they wouldn't try to move or finish their prey quickly, no matter how it wriggled. They would be patient and strong, and wait for the spirit to leave so that the prey could become meat, fit for eating. Once her jaws were clamped shut, nothing would open them.

The biggest risk now was not that the prey would escape, but that the other crocodiles would try to snatch it from her.

She glanced around her, but again, there was a strange emptiness to this part of the watering hole. Where *were* the others? They couldn't have failed to notice the disturbance in the water, could they?

The zebra twitched in her grasp, but weakly. Soon the water would flood its airways and it would be over.

And still, there was no sign of the others.

"They have come to me, child," said a deep, echoing voice. Gorge jumped and gave a great swipe of her tail to spin herself around in the water, though she had to drag the still-twitching zebra along with her. But there was no one behind her. And indeed, she realized, the voice hadn't *come* from behind her. It seemed to resonate through the water—or perhaps just inside her own head. . . .

"Let go of the grass-eater, my love," said the voice. It spoke sandtongue, but it didn't sound like a crocodile, or like any snake or lizard Gorge had ever known. It was deeper and somehow colder, as if it came from somewhere hollow, down inside the earth.

Gorge frowned. *I won't let go*, she thought. *This is my prey!*

"Gorge, I insist."

Gorge let go.

What? Why did I do that? she thought. She watched in shock as the zebra foal thrashed to the surface, gulped in air, and started to clamber unsteadily back up the bank, trailing blood from the tooth marks on its haunch, but very much alive. She tried to swim after it and grab it again, but she couldn't seem to move. Only after it was gone, lost in the vast air above, did she find her tail was back under her control. She spun in the water, snapping at nothing in case the invisible creature was nearby. *What did you make me do that for?*

"We have more important things to do now," came the reply.

Gorge snorted a stream of bubbles from her nose. More important than eating?

"Follow me, Gorge," the strange voice went on. "The others are waiting."

Gorge found her gaze fixed upstream, her tail moving slowly, pushing her through the curtains of long reeds. She wasn't sure anymore whether she was being forced to move, or whether she was doing it herself—she just knew this was the way she needed to go.

At last, she began to see ripples ahead. Tails and claws, all gathered along the bank at the far end of the watering hole. The rest of the bask were all there, from Swallow's gang of unruly hatchlings to elderly Crunch, who moved from her comfortable nest so rarely that her hide was slick with growing moss.

They were all facing the same direction, their heads up out of the water, as though something on the surface had caught their attention. Gorge swam up beside Feast, half expecting him to turn and greet her, but he was motionless in the water, like he was asleep, or watching a careless grasstongue wander too far from its herd.

Gingerly, Gorge raised her head from the water to see what the bask were staring at. But there was nothing there.

"My children," said the voice inside her head, and beside her Feast twitched, and Gorge knew that he'd heard it too. "The time of the sandtongue is here, at last. Grandmother needs you."

Gorge stared out with the rest of her kind, her gaze drawn up past the edge of the water, past the bank, past everything she had ever known, until it fixed on the purple shadow of the mountain on the far horizon.

"Your empty bellies do not matter now," said the voice. "Listen to Grandmother, and soon you will feast on all of Bravelands!"

CHAPTER ONE

"Moonflower! Grab my hand!"

Bramble reached desperately through the rain for his sister as she slid down the stony slope toward him. Moonflower flailed for him and gripped his arm. He tried to catch and steady her, holding on to a tree branch with his other hand. But her momentum was too strong and they both went tumbling, rolling down the hill. Bramble held on tight to Moonflower and squeezed his eyes closed, letting out yelps of pain as rocks and roots jabbed into his back and his shoulders. Finally they slammed into something hard and came to a stop in an ungainly heap against the trunk of a huge tree.

Moonflower managed to sit up, turning her face to the wet, black sky and letting out a groan of frustration.

"I hate this," she said.

Bramble knew just how she felt. He peered around the tree

trunk, but it was too dark to see their path down to the plains now. The mountain was almost behind them—the only home they, or their ancestors, had ever known—but the descent was hard, and there was nothing but wide, empty terror waiting for them at the bottom. Since he was a tiny baby, he'd known the old mantra: *Blood pools on the plains.*

But there was nothing for them up in the mountain either.

When Moonflower spoke again, it was in a small, almost hollow voice. "Do you think . . . I know you said you saw something, but . . . don't you think if we went back now, there's a *chance* she could be alive?"

Bramble sighed and sat down beside her.

What could he say? He was certain that her mother, Dayflower, was dead. He had seen the pain and terror in Dayflower's eyes as she'd been dragged back, into the depths of the vents that ran beneath the mountain. He had seen the thing dragging her—scaly coils like a snake, but unimaginably huge. Still, what snake was strong enough to overpower a gorilla?

"I'm sorry, but I know what I saw," he said gently. "We can't go back now."

"If there's even the slightest chance . . ." Moonflower gazed back up the slope that they'd just tripped and scrambled their way down. She opened her mouth to say more, but then froze, her breath catching.

"Bramble?" came a soft voice from the shadows.

Bramble would know that voice anywhere, and sure enough,

a moment later he spotted the shadowy shape of Apple Goldback, knuckling down the slope toward them.

"And Moonflower too! Thank goodness!" Apple said. "I
thought you might have hurt yourselves running down here."

Her voice was soothing, as calm and loving as it had always
been. Bramble swallowed and turned to stand awkwardly,
his heart torn between the urge to run toward her and the
urge to flee. Apple had always been a source of safety for him,
ever since she'd suckled him after her sister's death left him
orphaned. Right now he was bruised and tired and frightened, and Apple was the gorilla who could always make him
feel better. . . .

"Burbark wants to apologize, Bramble," Apple said, emerging from the shadow of the tree and stepping closer to the two
young gorillas.

Bramble saw the beseeching look on her face and her soft,
reaching hand, and then he saw the snakebite on her wrist. It
looked raw and wet, and not just from the rain that pattered
down all around them.

"There's been a misunderstanding," Apple cooed. "If you'll
just come back with me, Burbark will make it all right again,
I promise."

"Bramble," Moonflower said and grabbed his arm. "Don't
listen to her!"

"You're the *Brightback*, Bramble," Apple said. "Burbark
needs you to return, to take your rightful place as his heir.
The troop needs you."

Bramble looked down at the muddy ground, feeling the raindrops spatter across the back of his neck. With the troop it would be warm and safe, and perhaps Apple was telling the truth, perhaps it was all some awful misunderstanding, perhaps . . .

"The troop killed my mother!" Bramble turned to look at Moonflower. She looked back at him with sad eyes. "You're right," she added quietly. "There's no way she could have survived. And Burbark tried to *kill* us, too!" She turned her gaze back on Apple, and her expression hardened. "And you watched him do it."

Bramble looked at Apple, silently begging her to say something, anything, that would convince him Moonflower was wrong.

"Burbark was going to let you out of the vent soon," Apple said, waving her arm with its infected snakebite dismissively at Moonflower. "He lost his temper—you know how hard it's been for him. The prophecy at the Spirit Mouth would have shaken any leader! To be told that evil would spread from the very ground we stood on, and then poor Cassava . . ."

The sound of his brother's name seemed to sharpen Bramble's world back into focus.

"Burbark was responsible for Cassava's death!" he snapped and knocked Apple's hand away. Apple shrank back, looking shocked.

"How could you say such a thing?"

"Because Burbark was bitten before the Spirit Mouth

prophecy," Moonflower said. "*That's* when evil and madness came to this mountain."

"Come on." Bramble nudged her, and together they started to move away from Apple, trying to keep their footing without turning their backs on her. "We've got a job to do—we have to finish what Burbark stopped Cassava from doing. We're going to find the Great Parent and explain what's happening. If you really love the troop, Apple, you won't try to stop us."

"You're the mad ones," Apple said, shaking her head. "*Blood pools on the plains.* No gorilla has set foot on the plains since Kigelia first came to the mountain, and with very good reason! You'll die in that place!"

"Even so," Bramble said. "We're going."

Apple's outstretched, beseeching hand slammed down into the mud. Bramble jumped and instinctively reached for Moonflower's shoulder as Apple's kindly face drew down into a nasty glare.

"You're going *nowhere*," she snarled.

"Aah!" Moonflower squeaked, and Bramble felt her wrenched out of his grip. He spun around to see Lantana Goldback holding a wriggling, kicking Moonflower in her arms, and more of the Goldbacks and Blackbacks creeping between the trees. They were surrounded.

So much for safety, Bramble thought, desperately ducking under Woodnettle Blackback's grasping fists. He cast a despairing look back at Apple, but in her eyes there was no sign of the caring gorilla who'd raised him.

He reached for Lantana's arm, trying to prize it from Moonflower. Behind her, Groundnut Blackback loomed from the darkness, his face hard.

Moonflower gasped out, "Run!" and Bramble dodged back before Groundnut could reach him. He bared his teeth as Groundnut shoved past Lantana and stomped toward him, letting out a bellow that seemed to shake the mountain under Bramble's feet.

"I'll crush your skull before I see you abandon the troop!" Groundnut yelled. He raised both fists and brought them down in a wide arc that could smash rocks. Bramble rolled on his belly to avoid them and then scrambled back to his feet, almost slipping in the mud, catching himself with his toes on the edge of a big, mango-sized rock half stuck in the mud on the stony slope.

He looked up into Groundnut's furious, snarling face and hardly recognized the friendly Blackback he used to drop mangoes on from the branches of trees—his snarls then were all in fun, and there was nothing fun about the way he was coming for Bramble now.

Bramble leaned down, wrenched the rock from the mud, and hurled it at Groundnut's head. He couldn't help wincing as the rock struck home, perfectly in the middle of the Blackback's forehead, drawing a stream of blood and a howl of pain and fury.

Another howl joined his as Moonflower dropped from Lantana's arms, her teeth red with the Goldback's blood. Lantana cradled her elbow where Moonflower had bitten deep into the flesh. "Stop her!" she shrieked.

"Go!" Moonflower gasped, grabbing Bramble's hand as she leaped down the slope. Bramble spun and followed, his feet dancing over the rocks and his hand gripping his sister's so that at least if they fell, they would fall together. The hoots and bellows of the troop behind them were loud and furious, but Bramble tried not to listen, and he couldn't look back. He focused on the descent, swerving to avoid running into trees, leaping over rocks, skidding down patches of moss. They helped each other over the lip of a small cliff and dropped down into the darkness at the mouth of a cave, and Bramble paused for a moment, listening.

He could still hear the creaking of trees and the bellows of their troop, but they were distant now.

"Come on," Moonflower whispered. "We can't stop now."

"Not till we reach the plains," Bramble agreed. "They won't follow us there."

Because no gorilla has ever gone to the plains, he added to himself. *Because death is all that waits for us there. . . .*

But now there was nothing but death left on the mountain either.

They walked all night, even when the moon went behind the clouds and they couldn't see their feet beneath them, let alone the path ahead. The ground leveled out at last, which Bramble hoped was a good sign. Then, finally, he realized he could see once more. Gray mist wound between the tall trees as they grew sparser. His feet and hands ached, his back ached, and all he wanted to do was lie down and go to sleep.

Beside him, Moonflower's breath came in sighs and her steps dragged. But they had to press on. They had to reach the plains.

At last, a glistening golden light rose ahead of them, over the top of the mist, and they came to what Bramble thought must be the true end of the mountain—they were standing at the very edge of the tree line, at the top of a steep slope of rocks and brush that turned into rolling, grassy, empty plains. The silvery mist seemed to pool across the land, like a stream breaking its banks after heavy rain.

"Bramble," Moonflower whispered.

"I know," Bramble said. "We made it."

Moonflower tapped his shoulder. "No, look!"

She turned and pointed to a huge rock that sat between two trees, right at the edge of the forest, just like they were. Silver moss covered one side, so that it looked almost like . . .

"Kigelia!" Bramble gasped.

The rock looked just like a huge gorilla, his silver back turned to the plains, looking up into the mountain. Bramble almost thought he could make out the shapes of enormous fists planted in the ground, and two hollows in the rock that faced away from the sunrise so they collected shadow like great deep eyes. . . .

It was probably just a trick of the light, but Bramble still looked back at Moonflower with a new energy in his heart.

"This means we've come farther than any gorilla in . . . I don't even know how long. Generations," he said.

"Right," said Moonflower. She took a deep breath and

then knuckled slowly forward, away from the trees, so she was standing in the full dawn light. Bramble swallowed, cast one last look at Kigelia, and then padded out to join her.

"There's no turning back now," he said, and together they walked toward the plains.

CHAPTER TWO

Prance stared after the elderly baboon as he turned and shuffled away toward the big rock at the edge of the clearing. He moved slowly, as if his knees ached, and sank down to rest his back against the stone with a small grunt.

She trod the grass nervously with her hooves. She had expected the Great Father to be somehow . . . grander. She knew he was a baboon, and very old—this was Thorn, after all, one of the Three Heroes who had saved Bravelands all those years ago—but for some reason, she hadn't expected him to be so frail, or so . . . normal.

He peered up to the vulture that sat on the top of the rock.

"Fetch Mud for me, will you?" he asked.

The vulture gave Prance a last imperious glare, then took off and vanished into the forest canopy with a few beats of its great wings.

"Come, sit by me," said Great Father Thorn, patting the ground beside him. Prance hesitated for a moment, then sat, tucking her front hooves underneath her.

"Great Father," she said. "What did you mean when you said we were going to fix Bravelands? What else has been going wrong, other than . . ." She trailed off and bowed her head, looking down at the grass where her shadow ought to have been. Even now, it was hard to see that empty space and not feel afraid. She had lost her shadow, lost the Us that guided every gazelle through their lives, but she hadn't died. She'd thought she was cursed, abandoned by the Great Spirit. Her herd thought the same. But here she was, sitting in the shade beside the Great Father himself.

"You called?" came another baboon's voice, and Prance's gaze flashed to the other side of the clearing. Two more baboons had entered. The first was another male, almost as elderly as Thorn, with one eye that was covered over with a film of silver. He was followed by a young, scrawny female, who was playing with a small fruit, passing it from hand to hand. The old baboon stopped when he saw Prance and tried to draw himself up straighter, although he didn't get much taller.

"Mud," Great Father said, "this is Prance Herdless. She'll be with us here for a little while. Prance, this is Mud Starleaf, and his apprentice, Moth."

Prance had heard of the Great Father's Starleaf, and as Mud walked toward her she felt almost as intimidated as she had when she'd met Thorn. Every baboon troop had a

Starleaf, who the Great Spirit would whisper to through the stars and their special stones. Mud held himself with the kind of stiff dignity that she'd expected from Thorn, and his gaze was piercing as he stared at her through his one good eye.

"Hi," said the younger female, bounding up to Prance. "I'm Moth, nice to meet you!"

"Nice to meet you too," Prance said.

"Wow . . . it's really true," said Moth, circling Prance so that she had to twist her head to follow the baboon's jerky movements. "You have no shadow! That's so amazing!"

Prance almost laughed out loud. Nobody had ever called it *amazing* before. *Unnatural*, maybe. *Freakish.*

Moth sank down to sit beside her, looking at Thorn, as if they were two young baboons waiting for a story at the feet of an elder. Prance had never felt so welcomed, so quickly, and she instinctively dipped her head to hide her glowing expression from the baboons.

"It is certainly quite something," said Mud, with much less enthusiasm than his assistant had. He turned his bright eye on the Great Father. "I need to consult the stones about this."

Thorn nodded thoughtfully. "Something is afoot in Bravelands—exactly what, I'm not sure yet. Moth, will you go and fetch Gallant for me? His pride should still be nearby."

Prance startled at the mention of the lions. They hadn't hurt her when they'd caught her out on the plains and brought her to the Great Father, but she could still feel her muscles bunching to run. She forced herself to stay put as Moth scrambled to her feet and bounded out of the clearing.

"No harm will come to you, Prance," said Thorn, and Prance felt a little embarrassed that he'd seen her flinch. "While you remain at my side, I will do everything in my power to make sure you're safe. Gallant will be your personal protector, and no creature will bother you while you're with him."

I bet they won't, Prance thought. All the lions had been frightening, but Gallant was the pride leader, the largest and most threatening of them all.

A short time later, Moth loped back into the clearing with the big, fierce-looking lion right behind her. She watched his expression carefully as Great Father explained the plan to him, alert for any sign that Gallant's wide, terrifying jaws might be starting to salivate. But instead, she saw his eyes narrow as he looked at her, not in hunger, but something more like suspicion. He hesitated, ears flicking back for second, before bowing his great maned head to Thorn.

"I'll do as you ask," he rumbled.

"Excellent," said Thorn. He patted the lion on the shoulder. "I think you'll be good for each other."

Prance blinked at him, and then found herself meeting Gallant's eyes, seeing an equal lack of understanding reflected back at her.

What on earth does he think I can do for a lion? she wondered. But she should be polite.

"Thank you for saving me from the other pride," she said. "They would have killed me."

Gallant made a *humph* noise. "Great Father's orders," he said.

Thorn had wandered off and was talking quietly with Mud, and there was an awkward silence before Moth ran back to Prance's side and sat down, her eyes glinting.

"*So?*" she said, producing a small fruit from somewhere and taking a big bite. "Don't keep us in suspense like this, oh shadowless one. Tell us what happened!"

Gallant sat too, a little way away. Prance swallowed, still uneasy at the thought of him being so close, his predator scent telling every instinct she had left in her body to flee. But she focused on Moth's earnest, curious face and felt a little better.

She began to tell her story, starting with the day when she and Leap had found themselves Shadowless, but Prance had escaped death at the paws of the lame lion. She saw Gallant stir, his long tail smacking the ground. But he said nothing.

However, unlike Gallant or Great Father, Moth interrupted a lot.

"They just threw you out?" she gasped as Prance told of how she'd left her herd. "What did you do then?"

Prance told her all about the kind elephant who had counseled her at a watering hole, and she felt a glow of strange excitement when Moth identified Boulder as the brother of Sky, one of the other Heroes. She talked about how hard it was to lose the Us, the sense that bound every gazelle herd to one another. She talked about meeting Grassfriend and the zebra herd, saving Breezefriend from the lions, and becoming Prancefriend. Moth's eyes widened and lit up with every sentence, as Prance told her how nice it had felt to be accepted by creatures that weren't even your own kind, until Prance couldn't help but stop her story.

"What is it?" she said. "It's a pretty exciting story, but . . ."

"It's just that we have so much in common!" Moth declared. "No herd, no troop . . . friends in all sorts of places . . ."

"You don't have a troop?" Prance asked, her heart going out to the young baboon, even though she'd said it with a cheerful ease that didn't sound like she grieved it too much.

"My mother lives in a troop," Moth said. "But my father, Spider—well, he's a bit like you! He travels all across Bravelands by himself, making friends with other species, learning their ways. That's how I was brought up."

"Wow," said Prance softly. She couldn't quite imagine choosing that kind of life for herself. "And now you're with the Great Father, as an apprentice Starleaf?"

"Mud says I have great promise," said Moth, sitting up very straight. "If I apply myself."

Prance looked over at the elder baboons. Thorn had clambered up onto the top of his rock and was sitting there alone, hunched over, his eyes closed. Mud sat nearby on the ground, as if he was waiting patiently for something.

"Moth," Prance murmured, "the old does in the herd always used to say that the Great Father has the power to see through the eyes of other creatures. Is that really true?"

"Yep," said Moth. "He says it's a bit like swinging from branch to branch—oh, well, you wouldn't know what that's like, but that's what he says. He skips from creature to creature until he finds one that's looking at what he wants to know about, usually birds, because he understands skytongue and they can see so much. That's how he keeps track of all the important things happening in Bravelands. That's how he found you!"

Prance turned again to stare at the small baboon sitting on the tall rock. Could it really be true that his sight was out there somewhere, leaping from creature to creature? She remembered the vulture who had haunted her steps ever since she'd left Runningherd. Had that bird been carrying the Great Father with it, all along?

"Sometimes he's just taking a nap," said Gallant, without raising his chin from where it had dropped onto his paws.

"My eyes may be bad, Gallant," Thorn said, without opening them, "but my hearing is just fine."

Moth sniggered, but Gallant didn't seem to find it funny. His tail twitched and he got up, glaring up at the Great Father and then down at Prance.

"I need to hunt," he said. "I presume I don't need to be by the gazelle's side if she's here in the clearing."

Without waiting for an answer, he stalked off into the undergrowth.

Prance and Moth exchanged an awkward glance.

"I don't know much about lions," Prance said, "but . . . is he okay?"

"He—hmm. He reacts to things oddly sometimes. Doesn't like jokes. He's never gotten over losing his cub. It changed him."

"Oh," said Prance. "Sorry. How did the cub die?"

"We don't know," Moth said. "Poor little thing disappeared in the night. He was never found. And he was Gallant's only one," she added.

"Is that something to do with why the lions are here?" Prance asked. "I didn't think the lions followed the Great Spirit."

"Most don't. Gallantpride is different. They're descended from Fearlesspride. You know the story of Fearless? The lion raised by baboons?"

"I've heard about the Three Heroes," Prance said, feeling a sense of awe wash over her as she glanced up at the rock and remembered she was in the presence of one of the Heroes, even if she did think he might now be napping. "But I think some of it might not have been true."

"Well, I heard it from Mud, who was there," said Moth.

"Please, I'd like to hear it," Prance said.

Moth began to tell the story, gesturing widely with her arms as she recounted the tale of Stinger the baboon, who had been the False Father, of Sky and her guardianship of the Spirit, the herd of mismatched creatures, Titan the Spirit Eater, and the great fire. She threw herself down on the ground dramatically as she recounted the tragic romances of Thorn and Berry, Fearless and Keen, Sky and Rock, and finally the tale of Fearless's great sacrifice.

Despite the tragedy and danger in the story, Prance found herself feeling more and more settled as she sat and listened to Moth talk.

Here I am, she thought, *with a baboon who has no troop, listening to a story about a hero who was brought up with creatures he might have otherwise hunted and eaten.*

The name Prance Herdless no longer seemed quite so heavy. The place where her shadow should have been didn't catch her eye every time she turned her head. Her eyes started to droop closed. How long had it been since she had really rested, somewhere she felt safe?

"You can sleep here," Moth said, as Prance's head jerked up from where she'd let it droop for the third time. "Nothing bad will happen to you."

Gratefully, Prance let herself lower her head and tuck it down. The last thing she was aware of was Moth's soft paw patting her shoulder, and then she was fast asleep.

CHAPTER THREE

Chase slunk through the undergrowth, her ears flattened back against her head. Seek stumbled along just in front of her, his tail dragging in the mud behind him. Raindrops smacked into their fur and soaked the ground. Chase would have thought a little rain wouldn't trouble her, after their leap from the cave into the waterfall lake, but the water dripped into her eyes and ears, made everything glisten, and dampened the smells, so that she wasn't even sure exactly where they were.

"Chase!" came a roar from behind them, resounding across the mountainside even through the pattering rain. Chase flinched and nudged Seek to keep going.

Range was still after them, and she couldn't let him catch them. She didn't know much for certain right now, but she knew that.

Seek tripped over his paws and fell, and Chase seized his

scruff and pulled him back up, almost without missing a step.

"I'm sorry," she whispered. "We can't stop, okay? We just can't."

"It hurts," Seek groaned. But he managed to get back to his paws and limp onward, casting a fearful glance back over Chase's shoulder.

"I know," Chase said. She felt his pain each time she stepped on her own front paw, where the snake had sunk its fangs into her. There wasn't time to stop and inspect Seek's matching wound, but if it was anything like hers, it would be throbbing and burning, and turning darker even though the blood had stopped some time ago.

Chase whispered instructions to Seek, guiding him up along the low branch of a tree and down a rocky cliff on the other side, as once again the mountain rang with the echo of Range's roar. She imagined him bounding down the rocks from the waterfall cave, strong and fast, and the snakes slithering after him, hissing in their strange tongue.

Range had tricked them—tricked *her*. She'd trusted him.

Shadow had tried to tell her not to, but Chase hadn't listened. She'd thought Range would protect them from the hyenas and the gorillas. He'd seemed so nice. After the death of her mother, and everything she and Seek had been through, she thought that Range could be the answer. She thought Shadow was just jealous.

But Range had betrayed them, and Seek had almost died. Guilt throbbed along with the hot feeling in her paw, but even stronger than the guilt was the confusion.

Nothing that had happened in the cave made sense. What kind of leopard shared his den with hundreds of snakes and lured other leopards there to be bitten?

If Range had tricked her into bringing Seek so he could kill them himself and steal their territory, that would have been awful, but at least it would have been *natural*. Unlike the snakes that infested his den, or the way they seemed to do his bidding, or the way he spoke. *"Join us willingly, and serve the Silent One."*

She'd never heard of such a thing, not in all her days of listening to the chatter of prey or the stories of other leopards, or even from the strange talk of the gorillas.

He's gone mad, she thought. *The snakes are taking advantage of it somehow, to get him to bring them prey. There's no other explanation. Leopards do not serve anyone!*

There was another roar, and this one was closer. "I have your scent!" came the cry, Range's powerful voice carrying as if he was right behind them. "You should stop running!"

In front of her, Seek tumbled on, but his breath was coming in shallow gasps, and his steps were slowing. Chase shook herself.

"It's all right," she told him. "We're going to get out of this." She grabbed his scruff once more, lifting him right off his paws. Seek grunted with pain but didn't complain. He felt light and limp in her jaws.

Chase sprang into a faster run, still not as fast as she could move on four healthy paws and on familiar ground, but fast enough. She hoped. She was sure that if she could just make it a little farther, she *would* come out somewhere she would recognize, and then perhaps they could hide. . . .

She saw something move up ahead and skidded to a halt, her heart jolting, almost dropping Seek onto the ground in front of her.

More snakes! she thought. But after a second, she realized she'd only seen the shadow of a tree playing over the wet surface of a pile of sticks. She forced herself to run on, leaping over the sticks with Seek's tail dragging between her paws. She tried not to think about how easily it *could* have been another cluster of snakes, or how hard sandtongue creatures were to spot, because their scent was so faint. She also wouldn't let herself think about the fact that frequently snakes lived up in trees, or how easily one could drop down on her head.

I'm not afraid of snakes. I've never been afraid of them, she told herself. But things were different now. She knew that the sight of hundreds of them advancing on her at once, while Range watched, would haunt her nightmares until the day she went to the stars.

She could smell something strange, and after a few quick breaths she realized that it was Seek. The wound on his paw was already starting to fester. Her own wasn't so bad; the pain had dulled to a background throb and there was no sign of sickness that she could smell, but her heart squeezed as she drew breath after breath of that faintly rotten tang.

Then suddenly, she scented something else. Gorillas.

She heard snapping twigs barely a few leopard-lengths ahead of her and skidded to a stop, cursing Range and all snakes under her breath. The smell of Seek's snakebite had blocked out the scent of the gorillas until they were almost right on top of them. With a last look over her shoulder, she scrambled up into the branches of a tree. Seek mewled faintly with pain and confusion as she laid him in the crook of the tree, and she gave him a soft lick on his forehead before climbing along a branch and lying as flat and still as she could.

"What should we say?" said a female gorilla, emerging from the undergrowth and passing right below the branch where Chase was hiding.

"The truth. You know Burbark won't tolerate less."

Another gorilla passed underneath her, and another, and another. They were limping and sluggish, as if they'd spent all night running too. Some of them weaved as they trudged along, like they were dizzy as well as tired.

"We failed," one of them growled. He turned and punched a tree with his thick knuckles, and Chase flinched.

"They won't get far," another muttered. "Blood pools on the plains."

They went on grumbling to one another and stomping over the path Chase had been running along, and Chase's heart fluttered in her chest. If she was lucky, the sounds and scents of the gorillas would put Range off her trail! But she had to go, now, and be far away before he got to them. She snuck back down the branch and seized Seek's scruff in her jaws again. As she lifted him, he let out a mewl of distress, and the last of the gorillas turned. Chase hunkered back, as still as if she was stalking a skittish gazelle through long grass.

After a painful pause, the gorilla looked away and hurried up the mountain after the rest of its troop.

Chase slunk down from the tree, silent as a shadow, and broke into a run.

What can I do? Chase asked herself, over and over, as the smell from Seek's wound became worse and worse. *What am I going to do?*

She could think of only one thing. She had to find Shadow. He'd been right not to trust Range all along. When Seek had run away, Shadow had kept him safe—and when Chase came to get him, his reluctance to give the cub up had been because he was trying to protect Seek from Range, not steal him from her. Even if he hated Chase now, and she wouldn't blame him, surely he'd still want to help the sick cub?

But as she headed toward Shadow's den, she smelled something else that turned her stomach.

Hyenas, and blood. Lots of it.

The hyenas that had chased her over the river toward Range's den must still be around. It smelled as if they'd caught and killed something. She didn't have time to detour around the scents, so she pressed on, hoping she got lucky, hoping the hyenas were gone. . . .

Then she burst from the undergrowth to find herself within sight of the tree where Shadow had made his den, and stepped right into a splatter of blood and fur.

The ground was disturbed, dust kicked up and small plants torn from the earth, as if there had been a huge, terrible fight.

The place stank of hyena, but worse than that, it also smelled of leopard. Of Shadow.

No, Chase thought, pacing around the place where the fight had broken out. There were spatters of blood everywhere, and clumps of fur—the bristly gray and brown of the hyenas, and Shadow's distinctive soft black. The biggest blood spot ended in a long, dragging trail that led off into the bushes. Chase followed it until the trail vanished, with no sign of what had happened to the creature who'd been dragged away.

"No, Shadow . . . ," Chase groaned. *This is my fault. They probably followed my trail back here from the river.*

I was too proud to admit I could be wrong, and now . . .

What do I do now?

Chase was stumbling with exhaustion and grief as she finally found her way back to her own den.

Seek was a limp weight in her jaws, and when she put him down softly he lay there almost as if he was already dead, his eyes rolling back in his head. He was still breathing, his little belly hitching with shallow gasps. *But for how much longer?* Chase thought. *Will he ever open his eyes again?*

She curled up around him, tucking him close to her and draping her tail over him, licking the wound on his paw to try to clean it, though she could tell that the poison already ran too deep. She touched his nose with her own, and it felt cold.

"You'll be all right," she murmured. She couldn't tell whether he heard her. "I'm here. I'll keep you warm."

She wanted to shake him and beg him to wake up, but she

knew that that would be cruel. If this was his last night with her . . .

"Chase, you mustn't worry," Chase's mother had said before she left the den. She'd tried to reassure her, even though she must have known she was walking into danger. Because that's what a mother would do.

It had been only a few days since Prowl had died. Chase felt her absence now like a claw digging into her belly. Prowl had always said the time would come for Chase to live alone, like all leopards. A solitary, self-reliant life. The leopards' mantra, "trust only yourself," would become her mantra too.

But I'm not ready. Not yet. Not like this. Please, Seek, don't leave me here alone.

She forced herself to control her shuddering breath, pressed her nose to Seek's soft forehead, and closed her eyes.

"It'll be all right," she whispered to him. "You can go to sleep now. I won't leave you. I'll never leave you again. You'll see. Everything will be all right."

CHAPTER FOUR

The silvery mist that rolled across the plains was thick and cold. Bramble remembered the clouds that wreathed the top of the mountain, the way the tips of the peaks would be lost in them.

Maybe one of them fell out of the sky and landed on the plains, he thought.

Droplets of cold water coated his fur, and the world felt silent and eerie.

Moonflower walked beside him, keeping close so that they wouldn't lose each other in the thick fog.

A shape loomed from the gray mist, and Bramble grabbed Moonflower's arm, but then relaxed, with an anxious chuckle, as he realized it was only a tree—large and crooked, with a flat canopy. Even the trees were different, and more lonely, down on the plains.

Then a shrieking cry echoed overhead, and both of them

jumped and clutched each other's hands.

"What was that?" Moonflower whispered.

Bramble looked up, but apart from the distant burning orb of the sun, he couldn't see a thing.

". . . just a bird, probably," he said, trying to sound braver than he felt. "Come on. This mist can't go on forever."

But it didn't seem to be about to end, either. They walked for what felt like a very long time, trying to keep going in a straight line, over gently rolling ground that felt strangely soft and damp. Every so often something else would emerge from the mist in front of them—a rock, or a bush.

Bramble was watching something he assumed was a rock, walking right toward it, when it suddenly twitched into life and scrambled away into the mist. The two gorillas froze, gripping each other once again.

"What was that?" Bramble hissed.

Moonflower just shook her head.

They stayed there for a few minutes, breathing hard in the damp air.

"I don't like this," she said at last, through gritted teeth. "We have to find a way out."

Bramble nodded, but with every step they took, he felt less confident.

What if they had made a terrible mistake? What if that rock thing was a predator, and now it was stalking them, just waiting for its moment to leap from the fog, teeth and claws bared? What if they were doomed to wander aimlessly until they starved to death, or died of thirst, or just went mad? What if . . .

Beside him, Moonflower gasped, and Bramble jolted out of his thoughts and looked up.

"What?" he hissed, scanning the mist ahead of them. He couldn't see anything.

Moonflower didn't reply for a long moment, and then she whispered, "Mother?"

What? Bramble stared at his sister, and then out into the mist again. Still nothing.

Moonflower turned slowly, until she was staring back the way they'd come. "Do you see that?"

"No," Bramble said. "What is it? Where is it?"

"There!" Moonflower pointed. "You don't see her?"

The droplets in Bramble's fur prickled against his skin and almost seemed to freeze as a cold shiver ran down his spine.

Moonflower started to walk, slowly at first, and then knuckling into a run.

"Moonflower!" Bramble scrambled after her. "Slow down!" Panic seized him as he realized she was outpacing him.

"I see her!" Moonflower said, her voice already terrifyingly faint. "I can see my mother!"

"No," Bramble panted. He wanted to try to reason with his sister, to tell her it must be a trick of the light, but he couldn't get the words out before her shape faded in front of him, she leaped up and over a big rock, and she was gone into the mist. "Moonflower, wait!" Bramble yelled. He thought he heard a reply, but he couldn't make out the words.

He tried to put on a burst of speed, desperate to catch up, but they'd been walking all night, and he didn't think he could keep this up—

A shape loomed out of the mist.

Thank the Great Spirit, he thought. "Moonflower!"

But it wasn't Moonflower. The shape didn't move—he knew it couldn't have—but he came up on it so fast it almost seemed to lurch from the mist in front of him. Two great, dark, empty eye sockets above an enormous, gaping bone jaw. A skull almost as big as he was. Bramble shrieked and staggered back, tripping over something on the ground—more bones, from this creature's front leg where it must have fallen when it died.

He got back to his feet as quickly as he could, shaking all over. Was this some poor creature who had gotten lost in the mist, following visions like Moonflower? Was this his fate too?

"Bramble!"

Was that really Moonflower's voice, or was he hearing things now too?

After a moment, he shook himself. He hadn't imagined it; that really was Moonflower calling for him!

"I found it! Can you hear me? Follow my voice!"

With a last look back at the skull, Bramble homed in on where he hoped Moonflower's voice was coming from and started to make his way toward it. The ground sloped upward, grass slick with droplets of mist.

"I hear you," he called out.

"Up here!" Moonflower called back. Bramble's heart swelled as he realized her voice was louder now, and that the mist around him was turning pale, then white. As he came to the top of the hill it faded altogether, and he was standing, panting, in the sunlight at the top of a long slope of green and brown grass.

He stared down at the landscape, which seemed to roll on to the edge of the horizon, vast grasslands dotted with the occasional group of trees, or darker patches far away that might have been distant forests and hillsides, but the sun beat down so brightly that the scene was dazzling. He looked behind him and saw that they had been walking through a deep valley, in the shadow of the mountain. The mountain itself already seemed a long way away, its dark, forested slopes covered in cloud.

Moonflower was sitting on the sunny slope, her fingers toying with something at her feet. Bramble walked over to her.

"That was awful," he said, although now that it was over he felt much more cheerful about it. "I lost sight of you and ran right into a gigantic *skeleton*, and . . ."

As he got closer, he stopped talking. The plant at Moonflower's feet was a dayflower. Her mother's naming plant.

"I saw her," Moonflower said. "She was right in front of me. As clear as you are now."

"I didn't see anything," Bramble said. He sat down beside her, and she looked up at him with a sad smile.

"I know you didn't," she said quietly. "You're not the

Mistback. But I think I am. I saw my mother in the fog. She came to guide us out of the valley, and that means ... It means she's really dead."

Bramble shifted to sit closer to Moonflower, pressing his shoulder against hers, and was silent for a while. He didn't know what he could say. He knew what she was going through. His mother had died too, though he was too little to remember it. His brother had died, and that had made him the Brightback, heir to the leadership of the troop, a role he hadn't ever been sure he really wanted.

After a little while, Moonflower gave the dayflower's petals one last gentle stroke with her finger and then stood up.

"We should get moving," she said. "We need to cross all this to find the Great Parent." She gestured to the expanse of plain ahead of them.

For a while, walking in the sunlight was a huge relief. Even though they hadn't been lost in the mists for all that long, being able to see across the fields to the next copse of trees, the next ridge, all the way to the horizon, felt like a treat. The sky was so big. Bramble had never thought about the sky very much, except to trace the patterns of clouds and stars that peeked between the leaves of the trees. Here, you couldn't get away from it—it was a constant presence, a vast expanse of emptiness hanging over their heads, dotted with clouds so far away they could be as big as the mountain itself.

But soon enough, the endlessness of it all lost some of its novelty. The sun seemed so much hotter here, and the wind much harsher. Bramble licked his lips, but found they dried out again almost at once.

"I hope we find a stream soon," he said.

"It's so hard to tell where we should look for one," said Moonflower, shading her eyes. "Everything is so spread out. . . . I have a feeling we could walk right by one and we wouldn't know."

"It feels like the horizon is *moving*," Bramble said. "No matter how long we walk, it feels like we'll never get to the end of it."

"Let's stop for a minute by the trees," said Moonflower. "I need some shade."

Bramble nodded enthusiastically, and they put on a little more speed until they found themselves under the blessedly cool canopy of a copse of trees. Five trunks grew in a circle, right out of the dry earth, but the leaves were so tangled it was hard to tell which branches belonged to which trunk.

"There *must* be water somewhere under here," Moonflower said. "Trees and grass don't grow if there's no water. Mother told me that."

"But it must be very deep down," Bramble said. He put his palms to the ground.

Then he pulled them away again with a yelp.

The ground was shaking.

"What?" Moonflower asked.

"Put your hands on the ground, like this," Bramble said, and as Moonflower copied him, she looked up and met his gaze, wide-eyed.

The shaking was growing stronger. He could feel it through

his feet now too. He heard a soft rumbling sound, like faraway thunder, or the sound that came from the mountain vents. . . .

Is it the Great Spirit? he thought. *Is it trying to tell us something?*

But the rumbling grew louder, and above them the leaves of the trees began to rustle. Bramble straightened up and looked around them. The line of the horizon looked darker than it had been.

Not just darker . . . but closer.

"Something's coming!" he gasped, and by the time Moonflower had stood and turned, it was already much closer. Clouds of dust burst around it. It was coming much too fast, and the dark shapes in it were . . .

"They're animals," Moonflower said.

She was right. There were hundreds of them, dark-furred, with horns, pounding across the grass toward the two gorillas.

"We have to run," Bramble said. Moonflower grabbed his arm.

"No time, they're coming too fast. Up the tree!"

Bramble leaped and swung up onto the lowest branch and then reached down to pull Moonflower up after him. These weren't like the great tall trees on the side of the mountain— they were squat and wide. Bramble had climbed to the highest branch that would hold his weight in a matter of seconds. He clung on as tightly as he could and saw Moonflower in the crook of the branch beside him, bracing between two of the thinner branches. Then he looked down.

The stampeding beasts were almost on them. They were *huge*, twice as big as a Silverback gorilla. Their legs ended in big hard hooves, and they snorted and tossed their heads as they ran, spearing the air with the two great curling horns that sprouted from each skull. Bramble thought of the massive skeleton he'd seen in the mist.

"Hold on!" Moonflower cried as the first beasts thundered past the tree. The branch Bramble was lying on shuddered, bent, and dipped as the whole tree shook around him. Beast after beast passed below him, parting around the tree like a stream flowing around a rock. Bramble curled his head under his arm and shut his eyes, gripping on to the branch so tight that part of the bark cracked and flaked off under his fingers.

Finally, just as he was sure his grip would give out and the tree would throw him to the ground to be trampled by the huge beasts—if he wasn't speared on their horns first—the thunderous noise began to fade. He risked opening one eye and peered down to see the last few beasts streak by, snorting through the cloud of dust and swirling, falling leaves. He looked over to Moonflower and let out a grunt of relief to see her still clinging on to her branch, though she had also curled almost into a circle and squeezed her eyes closed.

"Well, hello there. What are you?" panted a low voice.

Bramble jumped and almost fell off his branch. He looked down to see one of the great beasts standing below him. It looked far skinnier than the rest, and he thought it was probably older—the thick brown hair that covered the others was thinning on this one, and around its mouth some of the hair had turned gray and was flecked with froth. Its flanks heaved with the effort of running.

"Are you monkeys?" it wheezed. "What happened to your tails? And why are you so large and swollen—did insects sting you?"

Bramble and Moonflower exchanged slightly offended glances.

"We're not swollen," Moonflower said. "We're gorillas. And what are you?"

"*Gor-ril-las.*" The creature seemed to roll the word around in its mouth. "Well, well. Never heard of such a thing before. I am a wildebeest, young *gorillas.* I suppose I should give thanks to the Great Spirit, for blessing me with one last new thing, before the end."

"The end?"

The wildebeest sighed and looked over its shoulder.

"I can't be doing all this running anymore," it said. "I'm too old. It's my time now. But you two young things should leave. The lions will be here soon."

"Lions?" Bramble gasped.

Golden like the sun, and twice the size of gorillas. Cassava's description rang in his head. *They have manes of black fur and tails that sting. And burning red eyes, and long pointed tusks!*

"Go on," urged the old wildebeest. "Before it's too late."

"Let's get out of here," Moonflower muttered and swung down from the tree in a few short leaps. Bramble dropped down beside her and looked up into the crusted black eyes of the wildebeest.

"Thank you," he said. "What about you?"

"I told you," said the beast. "It's my time." Its ears suddenly flicked back, and its eyes grew wide. "Go! Hurry!"

"Come on!" Moonflower grabbed Bramble's arm and pulled him away, and with a last look back over his shoulder, Bramble broke into a run. They knuckled across the exposed grass field as fast as their arms and legs could carry them and climbed up the next slope onto a rocky outcrop where long spears of grass grew up between the boulders.

They hunkered down beneath the grass and looked back. Bramble scanned the grassland for lions, and for a moment, he couldn't see any. But then something moved, the same tawny yellow color as the grass and dust. He saw the flicking of tails, and hunched, muscular shoulders as the creatures approached the tree. . . .

"Those are lions?" Moonflower whispered. "I thought they were supposed to have stingers? And red eyes?"

Bramble was about to reply when the lions broke into a sprint, and his words died on his tongue. These creatures didn't need glowing eyes or stinging tails to be terrifying. They were on the wildebeest in a moment, leaping with teeth bared and claws outstretched.

Bramble couldn't look. He dipped his head behind the rock and covered his ears, trying to block out the horror of the wildebeest lowing in pain. He hunkered there, trying not to think about the kind, curious creature who had made sure they were safe, or to wonder how long it would take. . . .

Moonflower put a hand on his shoulder, and he jumped. "We should go," she said.

Bramble looked up at her. Her face was strangely still, her

eyes wide and dark, and he realized that she hadn't looked away. She had seen it all.

"Don't look," Moonflower said. "Just walk. This way."

She scrambled down the other side of the outcrop, and Bramble followed, his heart heavy and his mind racing. The wildebeest had seemed so calm. What kind of place was this, that could make creatures just give up and accept a violent death?

It's really true, he thought. *Blood does pool on the plains.*

CHAPTER FIVE

Prance laughed and turned her head to the clear blue sky as she sprang over the grass. The Us thrummed in her blood, beating with the sound of the herd's hooves striking the earth. Skip pronked at her side, joy in every jump. Prance felt her horns cut through the air as she ran, the wind passing down her back. She heard the snorting laughter of the others and felt the Us guiding her steps. As one, the gazelle herd turned in a graceful arc, following the lines of the land, over a ridge and down through a valley, between two steep green-brown hills.

This must be how birds feel, Prance thought as they flowed across the land, passing over it effortlessly, but with the sound of rolling thunder. *Except they don't have the Us. I'm so happy to be back.*

"And we're so happy to have you back!" No gazelle said it, not even

Skip, but Prance felt it in her heart, through the Us, as if every member of the herd had spoken at once.

Prance and Skip jinked this way and that, their hoof strides in perfect unison, until suddenly Prance's hooves struck the ground and there was no matching thud from Skip. Silence filled the valley, and the sky was suddenly dark with storm clouds. The air was cold, and the Us was gone. Prance was all alone.

She slowed and turned around, then jolted as she saw that Skip was still there, but standing, motionless, at the head of the herd. They hadn't slowed or turned, they had simply . . . *stopped*. There wasn't a breath or a flick of an ear among them as Prance drew closer.

"Skip?" she said. "What's wrong?"

Skip met her eyes and opened her mouth.

Prance let out a honk of alarm as a long, forked tongue flicked from her friend's jaws. Skip's mouth moved, as if she was speaking, but all Prance heard was a thin, undulating hiss.

One by one, the herd opened their mouths, and the same hissing voice came from each one, echoing from the high walls of the valley. Prance didn't understand the words, but she felt the malice in their sandtongue speech. She tried to back away, but something was stopping her, and when she looked down, the grass of the valley floor had turned to thick, thorny vines that twisted around her legs and tore at her skin. She tried to pull her hooves free as the gazelle herd advanced on her. With every step, their bodies changed—horns pulling back into spines, hooves splitting into clawed feet, fur peeling away and revealing glistening scales. The awful half-sandtongue creatures crawled and staggered toward her. She writhed and stamped at the tangled vines, but the thing that had been Skip was almost on her, its face splitting as its jaws unhinged and opened to reveal teeth like a crocodile's. Desperate and horrified, Prance let out a cry of despair and butted at it with her horns.

She awoke and sprang up to stand in the same moment, as if the Us had sensed a predator and lifted her onto her hooves. She jabbed the empty air with her horns, saw that she was alone in the Great Father's clearing, and staggered back against the cool rock. Her heart was pounding and her flanks heaving with fear.

But she was safe. There were no terrifying lizard-gazelles here, only the rippling shadows of trees cast by the morning sun and the chattering of birds.

And the lion. Gallant lay nearby—not *too* nearby, but close enough that he could have reached her in a few bounds. His chin was resting on his front paws, but his eyes were open and staring at her. Prance shuddered before she could stop herself.

There was a rustling in the trees over her head, and a branch bounced and bent as Moth jumped, grabbed it, and swung for a moment from her hands.

"You okay, Prance?" she asked.

Prance nodded.

"Bad dreams," Gallant muttered. "She was honking in her sleep all night."

"Was I?" Prance said sheepishly.

"Like a herd of charging rhinos," said Gallant. He got to his paws, stretched, and yawned massively in a way that reminded Prance uncomfortably of the lizard-Skip's crocodile jaws. "I'm going to hunt. You'll be safe now that it's light." And without another word he turned and stalked out of the clearing.

"You weren't that loud," said Moth, dropping to the grass and pulling a face at the lion's retreating haunches. "You didn't wake me up. Are you all right, though?"

Prance sighed. "Gallant was right. I had bad dreams."

"Do you want to tell me about it?" Moth scratched behind her ears.

"Well . . . I was back with my herd. That wasn't the bad bit," she added. "It was wonderful. I was with Skip, and everything was normal—I had the Us again."

"Wow," said Moth. She pulled out a small insect from her neck fur and rolled it between her fingers, looking thoughtful. "Is it nice? The Us, I mean. It must be nice to have a connection like that."

"It was," said Prance.

"Oh—sorry. We don't have to talk about it if you don't want to."

"No, it's all right." Prance sat down and nibbled on a patch of dewy grass at the base of the tall rock before she spoke again. "It's wonderful. It's just . . . like always having a friend by your side. It's like always knowing the answer, whether it's time to run or sleep or feed . . . I miss it," she admitted. "How do most animals cope, relying only on themselves all the time?"

Moth shrugged and popped the insect into her mouth. "Just do. Don't know any different, I suppose. Although my father claimed he'd had the Us once."

"What? But . . ."

"Yeah, I know. I don't think he *really* did. He says things like that all the time. I think he just lived with some gazelles for a bit and learned their habits. He's really good at *imagining* he's other animals, that's all."

I suppose that's what I was doing in my dream, Prance thought. *Imagining I was a normal gazelle again . . .*

"Well, it was nice while it lasted," she said. "But then everything went wrong—I lost the Us, and when I turned around, the herd was changing into these . . . these *snake* things. They were yelling in sandtongue, and coming toward me, and . . ." She trailed off with a shudder.

"Sounds weird," said Moth. "Maybe you should tell Thorn. He's really wise about things like that."

Prance opened her mouth to say it was just a bad dream and not worth bothering the Great Parent with, but then she stopped. Perhaps Moth was right.

When Thorn arrived he was with Mud, the two elderly baboons walking with their heads bent together, deep in conversation. Mud stopped talking when he saw Prance and gave her a wary nod. Then he and Moth both helped Thorn up onto the top of the rock, where he shuffled until he seemed comfortable. Prance waited patiently until he was settled and then stepped forward.

"Great Father," she said, "There's something I'd like to ask you about. I had a dream. . . ."

"It's not a good time right now, Prance," said Mud before Thorn could reply. He gestured over Prance's head, and she turned to see a strange sight gathering at the edge of the clearing—a group of creatures, waiting with their gaze fixed on Thorn's seat on top of the rock. There were meerkats climbing up a rock to get a better view, and a flock of small birds perched along a low branch, with pale gray bodies and black-striped faces. The birds cheeped and sidled along the branch as a full-grown giraffe bent its head to duck into the clearing.

"They're here to ask the Great Father for advice," Moth whispered to Prance.

Mud crossed the clearing and began to speak with the creatures, gesturing first to the giraffe. The giraffe had to lower its head almost to the ground to hear him.

"We'll talk later, Prance," Thorn assured her. "Is that all right?"

"Of course, Great Father," Prance said, bowing and stepping back to give the great tall creature room as it lolloped into the center of the clearing.

"Great Father. Thank you for seeing me." The giraffe bent his front legs and bowed deeply to Thorn. "I'm from Dawn Herd; my name is Skywatch. Great Father, something is wrong with my herd. It's our leader, Broadsight. It's like—like he's lost his mind! We don't know what to do."

Prance realized that although the giraffe was fully grown, or nearly, he was quite young. She could sense his nervousness in the way he spoke, short statements strung together in a hurry, as if he was afraid that Thorn would dismiss him at any moment.

"I know Broadsight," said Thorn, leaning forward and frowning. "The last time I saw him he was in good health—what do you mean by 'lost his mind'?"

Skywatch straightened up, and Prance saw his huge throat constrict as he swallowed. "He's just not talking like himself. It's as if he woke up one day as a different giraffe. He doesn't recognize his own kin half the time. He really cared about the herd, but now it's like he's lost interest. He's always talking about leading the herd away somewhere."

"Strange. Did anything happen to him that could have caused this?" Thorn asked. "Perhaps he hit his head, or lost someone dear to him?"

"No, nothing like that." Skywatch shook his head vigorously, which made Prance feel strangely dizzy. "I mean . . . he does have a lame leg. I think something bit him. Could that be it?"

The young giraffe looked toward Mud, who scratched his chin. "No, I don't think so. Even if it was a venomous bite, it shouldn't be enough to addle the mind of a fully grown giraffe."

Thorn asked Skywatch a few more questions, but Prance found herself distracted.

A venomous bite . . .

The face of the sandtongue monster that had been Skip flashed in front of her eyes, and she felt the hairs on her back prickle. Could it have been a snakebite? Could that have done something to the giraffe leader? She wanted to ask Skywatch, but interrupting the Great Father was unthinkable. Perhaps she'd be able to ask him later.

"Is there any way you can get Broadsight to come see me himself?" Thorn asked.

"I don't think so," Skywatch said miserably. "He won't listen to us, and he gets furious if anyone suggests anything's wrong. Like I said, he's getting obsessed with the idea of moving the herd. We've been trying to dissuade him—he wants to go to the *mountain*, of all places! When there're plenty of juicy leaves in our own territory! I just don't know what to do. Maybe . . . maybe you could come with me to the herd and see him there?" Skywatch gave Thorn a pleading look.

"I'm sorry," said Mud. "The Great Father wishes he could come, but he is an old baboon, and he is needed here, for all the animals."

Skywatch's wide eyes narrowed. "Well—what am I supposed to do, then? What use is a Great Father who can't help us?"

"I'm afraid Mud is right," said Thorn, much more gently. "I'm not well enough to travel to your herd at the moment."

"The Great Father can't be expected to solve every little problem in person," Mud added. Thorn cast him a look that Prance couldn't quite read and went on.

"I remember Broadsight as an honorable, dependable leader," he said. "But it sounds like his leadership might have come to its end. Perhaps it would make sense to elect a new leader."

Skywatch's frown softened into a look of resignation. "Thank you, Great Father," he said. "I will take your words back to my herd."

The young giraffe turned and lolloped out of the clearing, looking downcast. Mud waved to the three meerkats, who sensibly waited until the giraffe had left the clearing before skittering toward the rock. Prance's ear twitched as she heard Thorn mutter under his breath.

"You're getting grumpy in your old age, Mud."

"I am not," Mud muttered back. "I just value your time, that's all. Did you want to walk to Dawn Herd? You could have said so."

Thorn sighed but didn't argue.

"Great Father!" The meerkats had reached the bottom of the rock, and they were rearing up and down and chattering over one another. "Great Father, Great Father, our kits!"

"Our kits have gone!"

"They've gone!"

"Great Father!"

"It was those traitors—"

"—scum! Kit-killing scum!"

"The Yellowhill troop, they stole them!"

"Hardly fit to be called meerkats . . ."

"That termite mound was on *our* territory."

"It was *ours*."

"We've been at war—"

"But we never thought—"

"Our kits!"

"They've broken the Code!"

"Only kill to survive!"

Prance frowned. Following the meerkats' chatter made her horns ache. She cast a glance at Moth, who seemed upset about the kits but was also squinting slightly as she tried to make sense of it all. Thorn listened calmly, seemingly letting it all wash over him until he felt he understood, at which point he stood up on two legs with a grunt, holding his front paws up in the air, and all the meerkats immediately fell silent. Prance stared in amazement, wondering how Thorn had discovered this trick. He must have been dealing with meerkats an awfully long time.

He pointed to the leftmost meerkat.

"Jink. Are you quite certain it was the other troop who took the kits?"

"Who else?" chirped the meerkat called Jink. "They're our enemies!"

"Yellowhill has gone too far this time," piped up another meerkat, but at a glare from the other two she shrank back again. Apparently when the Great Father chose a speaker, even the meerkats took that seriously.

"Hmm." Thorn scratched his nose. "I cannot make a judgment until I know both sides of the story. I will send an envoy to investigate. I promise you, we will find the truth, and if they have truly broken the Code, there will be consequences."

"Consequences," repeated the middle meerkat with quiet satisfaction.

"Thank you, Great Father," said Jink. "We'll look out for your envoy."

The three meerkats turned and scampered away. Prance heard them muttering as they went, repeating *Yellowhill* and *consequences* to one another. She wondered who Thorn would send as his envoy, and what they would find.

As the meerkats left, Prance noticed that more animals had gathered around the clearing. There was a cheetah, which made Prance's heart race—although less now than it had when she'd first met Gallant—a warthog, a young red-tailed monkey, and an elderly-looking hyena with scars all across her face, who the others were staying far away from.

But the next petitioners to approach Thorn's rock were the flock of small black-and-white birds she had seen earlier. She watched in awe as they flew up to perch beside the Great Father, twittering in their strange language. Thorn listened attentively, nodding just as he would do if they had been speaking grasstongue.

Thorn turned to Mud. He looked concerned. Had the little birds been telling him about problems as serious as Skywatch's and Jink's? But she also saw that he blinked more than he had before, and he took an extra few labored breaths before he spoke.

He's tired, she thought. *He is so very old, and there are so many more animals who need him. . . . I wish I could do something to help.*

"The plovers tell me something very strange," he said to Mud. "They say that the crocodiles have been *eating* them."

Why is that surprising? Prance wondered. She leaned down to ask Moth, but Moth obviously knew what she was about to say.

"Plovers and crocodiles usually live together," the young baboon said. "The plovers eat the leftover food from between the crocodiles' teeth."

"And the crocodiles don't eat them?"

"No! They get their teeth cleaned, and the plovers get fed. They're friends! As much as you can be friends, when you're a skytongue and they're a sandtongue. It's been like that, for . . . well, it's *always* been like that." She looked just as worried as Mud and Thorn. "I've never heard of a crocodile eating a plover before."

"Crocodiles are not Bravelands' most considerate creatures," Mud said. "But still, that does seem strange."

The birds were chirping again, and Thorn was listening intently and nodding.

"I need to see this for myself," he said. "I'll travel in my mind and find a way to observe."

The birds flew away, and Thorn looked down at the gathered creatures in the clearing. Prance saw him sigh and steady himself with one paw on the rock.

Mud clearly saw it too. He met Prance's eyes and said, "The others will have to wait. Will you tell them, Prance?"

"Oh! Of course," Prance said. She drew herself up and started to approach the waiting animals, pointing her horns proudly to the sky. Even the hyena and the cheetah didn't seem quite so scary. She was doing this for the Great Parent. They wouldn't dare hurt her. "I'm sorry," she said. "The Great

Father has very important things to do, and he needs his rest."

"What?" the hyena snapped. "I came all this way!"

"This is outrageous," grumbled the warthog.

"But my problem is urgent!" said the monkey.

"All our problems are urgent." The cheetah stretched and fixed Thorn with a suspicious look over Prance's shoulder. "If the Great Father can't help us, we'll have to sort it out ourselves." He turned and stalked away into the trees.

"If Great Father can't help us, maybe the Great Spirit should choose someone else," muttered the warthog.

Prance's ears flicked back in distress. "I'm sure if you come back tomorrow . . . ," she began, her voice shaking a little.

"Will he be any younger tomorrow?" the monkey snapped. She jabbed a finger into Prance's chest. "You tell him, young gazelle. We need a Great Parent who can do his job."

The monkey and the warthog both turned and walked away, grumbling to each other. The hyena sat down and scratched behind her ear with her back leg.

"I'll be here," she said, and settled down at the base of one of the trees, tucked her front paws under her, and seemed to go straight to sleep.

Prance backed away and headed back to Thorn on jittery hoofsteps. What was she going to say to the Great Father? How could she tell him that the petitioners were upset with him? That they thought he was too old to be Great Parent?

She reached the rock just as Mud and Moth were helping Thorn climb down, standing ready to catch him in case his fingers slipped.

"G-Great Father," she said. "I told them you couldn't see them, and . . ."

"How badly did they take it?" Thorn said, lowering himself to the floor with a grunt.

"Not—not well," Prance said.

"It's all right, my friend. I know that they say I'm too old and decrepit to be a good Great Father anymore. Perhaps they're right."

Prance gave Moth an alarmed look, but Thorn went on.

"I think I should call a Great Gathering. I should reassure everybody. Make it clear that whatever my physical limitations, I am still their Great Father, and they can trust me."

"Good idea," said Mud firmly. "They have no idea how hard you work for them. You get some rest, and I will make the arrangements."

Thorn yawned and hobbled off to climb slowly up a nearby tree.

Prance watched him go, thinking hard.

"Mud," she said finally. "I want to help the Great Father. And I had this dream. . . ." She paused as Mud turned to fix her with a hard stare. Behind him, Moth nodded her head and gestured for Prance to go on, so she did. "It's just that I have a theory. It might be nothing. But if Broadsight the giraffe leader was bitten by something venomous, and the crocodiles have started being more violent, what if there's some connection to the sandtongue creatures? In my dream, my herd turned into sandtongues and attacked me. Maybe they had something to do with the missing kits, too?"

Mud snorted. "And you think this because you had a dream?" He shook his head. "Leave these things to the old and wise, young gazelle. It might be better if you stayed out of the Great Father's way."

And with that, he turned and hobbled away. Prance stared after him and then hung her head. Perhaps he was right. After all, she'd almost forgotten she was here only because she'd lost her shadow. Why would the Great Father want advice from an ill omen?

She felt about as tall as a blade of grass.

CHAPTER SIX

Chase jerked awake, and at once she reached out a paw to touch Seek, shuddering with fear that she might find him cold and still beside her.

But her paw found nothing except cool earth.

She sat up, her ears pinned back, and called out, "Seek?"

There was no answer but a small snuffling sound. Her eyes adjusted to the dim light of the den, and she gasped. Seek was there, on the other side of the den. Not just alive but awake, licking at the snakebite wound on his leg.

Joy flooded her heart, and she scrambled up to her paws. "Oh, Great Spirit, Seek! Are you all right?"

She ran over to him and nuzzled him hard enough to knock him over, rubbing her cheeks against his and licking the soft fur under his chin. It was only when he snarled and batted at her nose, his sharp little claws prickling in her fur, that she realized he hadn't replied. She drew back.

"Oh, Seek, I'm so sorry! Did I hurt you?"

Seek hissed, backing up into a corner of the den on shaky paws. Some of the joy drained from Chase as she saw the distrust in his eyes.

But he's alive! she told herself. *Everything else, I can live with.*

"Can I see the bite?" she asked him. "I can help you clean it."

"No! It's fine!" Seek snarled.

"Oh—I'm sorry," Chase said. "It's all right. You're going to be all right."

Once again, Seek didn't reply. He just sat leaning against the wall of the den, licking at his bite. Worry prickled behind Chase's ears. What had gotten into him? Was he in pain? Or maybe he was still terrified from their ordeal?

"I'll get us something to eat," she offered. She was ravenous herself. Running from Range and his snakes had been bad enough, but she felt like the night she'd spent holding Seek and fearing the worst had emptied her out. Now that she could see he was all right, she thought she could eat an elephant.

"I'll be back soon," Chase said softly. Seek just glared at her and settled into a ball of angry-looking fluff in the corner of the den.

The sun was already high in the sky as Chase slipped out of the hollow beneath the tree and sniffed carefully around the den. There was no scent of Range or the snakes.

She jumped at shadows more than once as she made her way between the trees. The dappled sunlight on the branches looked just like snakes, and the breeze made them shift as if they were alive. But she slowly began to relax, at least enough to focus on searching for the scent of prey instead of obsessively checking for any sight or scent of Range. She stalked along the trail left by a young bushpig, drooling at the delicious smell, and caught it while it was distracted by snuffling in the roots of a tree for its own meal. Bushpigs were hardy, prickly things, and strong too, but Chase was stronger and hungrier. She ended the short struggle with a bite to the back of its neck and started to drag it back toward the den.

Then, even through the delicious smell of the bushpig, she caught a scent that made her fur prickle. Not Range, but hyena.

As quickly and quietly as she could, she pulled her prey up into the branches of a nearby tree and began to make her way back home that way. It was harder, with a heavy pig in tow, but Prowl had taught her well. It was worth an awkward stretch and leap from one tree to the next, with the prey clamped firmly in her jaws, to keep out of harm's way. The last thing she needed right now was to get into a fight.

The hyena scent was muted from up in the trees, but Chase could still smell it—and it was getting closer. It was definitely between her and home. She paused, considering the idea of trying to detour around it, and then suddenly realized she could *see* the hyena, through the undergrowth below. It was just one, and it was lying awkwardly against a rock.

Treading so lightly it would have made her mother proud, Chase snuck along a branch and managed to clamber into the next tree and get a better look.

The hyena was female, and wounded. She was worrying at her hind leg, in a way that reminded Chase uncomfortably of Seek back in the den, and growling and snapping at the flies that were persistently trying to crawl over the wound.

The tree branch beneath Chase gave a creak, and Chase crouched back, but the damage was done. The hyena's head snapped up, and she let out high-pitched growl as she saw Chase.

"Leopard," the hyena snarled. "Thinking of finishing me off? Come down here and try it, you'll feel my teeth!"

"I've no intention of coming down there," Chase replied. She backed up closer to the tree trunk, where the branch was thick and safe to linger on, and sat on her haunches.

"My pack-mates will be here any moment," muttered the hyena. "Better be gone by then."

Chase shook her head at this obvious lie. Hyena packs didn't look out for one another like wolves, but they wouldn't leave one another alone like leopards either.

"If your pack comes back, it'll be to eat you," she said. "That's what I heard. Hyenas are happy to make a meal of their own kind, given the opportunity. Isn't that right?"

The hyena gave Chase a look of disgust and anger that Chase suspected meant she was right.

"They wouldn't dare," she said. "You mock me, but if I could reach you, you'd be scraps for the vultures. The other leopard, that arrogant male with the black fur, he tried to take me on, and he regretted it."

"Shadow?" Chase gasped before she could help herself. "You fought Shadow?"

"Do I look like I give a gorilla's toenail for your stupid names?" the hyena spat. "It was a leopard, but it was black."

Chase swallowed down the fear that was rising in her throat. "What happened to the leopard? Did you . . . did you kill him?"

Please, she thought. *Please, Great Spirit, I know you've done one miracle for me already today and brought Seek back to me, but please let Shadow be okay. . . .*

"Yes," said the hyena. Chase's heart skipped a beat. But then she saw the look on the hyena's face—the defiant, narrowed eyes and slight smile.

"No, you didn't," Chase snarled back. "Tell me what really happened!"

The hyena rolled her eyes. "I didn't see. He was as good as dead by the time he did this to me and then dragged himself off. My pack-mates went after him, so he's dead now, you can count on it. Now, if you wouldn't mind, I'd like to be left alone. If I'm about to die, I don't want to do it looking at a leopard, if it's all the same to you."

Chase suddenly felt a strange pang of sympathy for this hyena. She'd been left here by her pack, either to get better or die alone.

But there were more important things to worry about right now.

"Tell me which way they went, and I'll go," she said.

The hyena squinted up at her and licked her lips. "Give me your prey, and I'll tell you."

Chase hesitated, but only for a moment. She could get more prey, but Shadow wouldn't wait. It might already be too late.

"Deal," she said. She picked up the bushpig, walked out onto the branch, and dropped the creature down right beside the hyena. The hyena sniffed it and started drooling.

"Very well. They headed that way." She jerked her head awkwardly, indicating the trees behind her. "Down the hill, toward the stream."

"Thank you," Chase said, then took a running jump and sprang over the hyena's head into a tree in the direction of the stream.

"Don't thank me," sighed the hyena, dragging the bushpig toward her. "The others will just kill you too."

Chase tried not to think about that. She made her way down to the ground, where the hyenas and an injured Shadow would have most likely been running. She sprinted between the trees, her muzzle open, tasting the air for any trace of her friend. If she could still call him that after what she'd done.

It didn't take long to find the trail. There was a strong smell of hyena, a faint smell of leopard, and a very strong smell of blood. She put on a burst of speed and leaped across the shallow stream. On the other side, she started to see the drops of dried blood, and she followed them at a fast slink, her ears pinned back and her tail long and stiff behind her.

She told herself she had to be ready. To face the hyenas . . .

or to face Shadow's corpse. She wasn't ready for either.

She came upon the tree so suddenly, she almost ran into it. The trail of blood led up the trunk, and in the crook of two branches there was a bundle of black fur, a tail and one limp paw dangling loosely.

Then the bundle breathed, and Chase gasped and kneaded the ground in front of her in excitement.

"Shadow! You're alive!"

Shadow lifted his head and turned it slowly to face her. Chase felt as if she'd plunged into the cold stream as she saw that only one of his eyes opened—the other was swollen shut, a pair of crusted puncture wounds right above it. Shadow glared at her through his one good eye and sniffed.

"You," he said coldly. "Go away."

Chase cringed back, her tail tucked between her legs. "I'm so sorry, Shadow."

"Where's Seek?" Shadow said, narrowing his eye.

"He's safe," Chase said quickly. She sighed. "I'm sorry. It's my fault the hyenas found you, I think they followed my trail—"

"I know," Shadow cut her off.

"You were right about everything," Chase said. Shadow opened his sore mouth to speak again, and Chase shook her head. "Just let me speak. I need to tell you that you . . . I was wrong about Range, and wrong about you. You just wanted to keep Seek safe, and I stole him. He's my cub, but that doesn't make it right to treat you like I did. And then we were chased by the hyenas, and I went to Range's den, and . . . you were right all along. He betrayed us."

"What?" Shadow said. "How?" He started to shift his weight, pulling up his limp paw and trying to stand. He wobbled on three paws as he tried to turn on the branch, his sides heaving with the effort.

"No, don't . . . ," Chase said. "Don't move!"

"Don't tell me what to do!" Shadow hissed.

"But you'll fall!"

"What do you care?" Shadow snarled at her. "You ran off and led those hyenas right to me! It serves you right if Range atta—"

He broke off with a yelp as his back paw slipped. He scrambled for purchase but fell, dragging his claws down the trunk to slow his descent. Chase ran up to the trunk and tried to break his fall, and both of them landed on the ground in an ungainly heap of fur.

"I'm . . . fine . . . ," Shadow panted, even though Chase could see he was definitely *not* fine—his breath was shallow and it sounded like it hurt, and when he grunted and pushed himself off her back, his flanks trembled with the effort.

From up the slope, Chase heard the unmistakable squeaking laughter of a hyena. Then a second joined it, and a third.

"Shadow, we have to go," she said.

"Then go," Shadow spat. "I was fine before you came along. I don't need your help."

"No!" Chase nudged at him, trying to be gentle, but almost

unbalancing him anyway. "I'm not leaving you again. Hate me all you want, but *stand up.*"

Shadow groaned and pressed his good paw into the ground, levering himself unsteadily up to stand on his three good paws. The hyenas laughed again, closer now, the rapid grunts rising in pitch as the hyenas grew more excited for their meal. Shadow looked at Chase, the pain that clouded his gaze starting to clear as terror overtook it.

"Go," Chase whispered. Shadow nodded and started forward, flinching, but not falling down. Chase moved behind him, to let him set the pace and so she could turn and fight if she had to. She wouldn't die here, but she wouldn't let them get Shadow. Not again.

They slipped into the undergrowth and made their way achingly slowly toward Chase's den. A few times Shadow wobbled and looked like he would fall, and Chase leaped forward to catch his shoulder against her own and prop him up. He growled the first two times, but stayed silent after that.

Chase could tell when the hyenas reached the tree where Shadow had been. Their pursuit stopped, and though she couldn't make out the words, she could hear a baying conversation between several hyenas.

Maybe the scent will confuse them, she thought, a tiny hope growing in her heart. *There's so much blood and fur. Maybe they won't know which way we went.*

Sure enough, the noise faded into silence after a while. Shadow's desperate breathing slowed, and he wobbled and fell less often. At last, they made it back to the den beneath the tree. Chase went in first, suddenly afraid that Seek might be gone, or that the bite might have gotten worse while she was away. But Seek was in the same place she'd left him, curled up in the corner of the den, still licking at his bite wound. When he saw her enter, he curled even tighter into himself and his fur puffed up. The look he gave her almost stopped her in her tracks, but she reminded herself that he was probably in pain. Just like Shadow.

"I've brought Shadow with me," she told him. "He's been wounded by the hyenas, so he'll stay here for a bit. Is that okay?"

She was expecting Seek's frown to lift at this news. After all, Seek liked Shadow. He'd seemed like he didn't mind the idea of living with him, when she'd gone to fetch him back. *It'll be nice for them,* she thought. *They can sit in the den and hate me together.*

But if anything, Seek's angry expression deepened as Shadow limped into the den.

"I'm glad you're okay, Seek," Shadow said, flopping down near him.

"I'm not," Seek hissed. "I'm hungry, and I hurt." He turned to glare at Chase. "You were supposed to be hunting. It's hard enough to feed two of us, and now we have three. What were you thinking, bringing him back here?"

Chase was stunned. She saw Shadow's ears slip back in distress as the cub spoke. She couldn't blame him.

"He's hurt, Seek," she said. "And it's my fault. Come on, it's *Shadow.* I couldn't just leave him out there to be eaten." She said it with a half-chuckle, trying to lighten the mood.

But Seek's eyes were cold and his voice flat as he looked at Shadow and said, "I don't see why not."

Chase shivered.

What has gotten into him? He was sweet and kind, but now . . . What's happening to my cub?

CHAPTER SEVEN

Bramble tried to focus on the ground in front of him and the distant shadows of trees, but as he and Moonflower walked across the vast plains, his thoughts still echoed with the painful lowing of the wildebeest, and even worse, the moment when it had stopped.

As the sun had risen, and the trails of mist that still crossed the ground had burned away, it had become incredibly hot. Moonflower reached back to help him clamber up and over a rock outcrop, and Bramble half hoped he would see trees on the other side, or the shade of a valley, but instead there was just more scrubby grassland. He squinted into the brightness and made out some bushes and a single tree in the far distance, but it was small and its branches were bare.

Bramble tried to focus on the practicality of their mission: find the Great Father. Surely, if they kept walking, they would find a creature who knew where he lived.

But it was hard to think about anything but the lion attack and the sticky feeling of his tongue as it got drier and drier. He licked his lips, and then wondered if it was a waste of spit. He had never been this thirsty. In the mountains there was shade and lush green foliage, and he had always taken them for granted. He'd never even wondered what a world would be like without them. He didn't think he liked it.

What if we've made a terrible mistake? he thought, not for the first time. *What if we're going to dry out and die here before we ever find the Great Father? Maybe Apple was right. . . .*

He couldn't help turning to look over his shoulder. The mountain was nothing but a looming shadow on the horizon now. His heart ached as he realized how far they'd come, and how hard it would be to make it back. . . .

"I miss it too," said Moonflower in a slightly rasping voice. "But we have to remember why we're doing this. Dayflower died so that we could bring the Spirit Mouth's message to the Great Parent."

"I know," said Bramble and set his gaze back on the plains ahead of him. "I just . . . I never thought I'd say this, but I miss the troop. I miss Apple and Groundnut. I even miss Burbark. The way they used to be, before . . . all of this."

Moonflower put a hand on his back. "That feeling is why we're here. So that maybe we can get them back."

Bramble took a deep breath, even though it dried his throat out even more. "You're right. Let's go."

They walked on and found themselves pushing through

dry grasses. Bramble's knuckles were brown with dusty earth, and the grasses prickled his face as he wove between the tufts. He tried to fix his eyes on the horizon. Somewhere over there, there was *something* different, dotted dark patches that could have been trees or rocks or even animals. But a strange haze was rising from the ground, like the steam escaping from the Spirit Mouth. He kept thinking they must be about to find the source of it, but every time he looked up again, it seemed to have moved farther away.

Suddenly, a shadow passed over Bramble, and then another, and then the whole field was swarming with shadows. He looked up and gasped. Flocks of birds, of several different types, were all flying together across the plains in the same direction he and Moonflower were walking. Huge bald-headed vultures, many small black and white and brown birds Bramble couldn't identify, birds with long legs and a distinctive fan of black feathers streaming behind their heads, and a few with startlingly bright orange heads and green wings and bodies. He saw hawks and buzzards, flying alongside the small birds they would usually hunt for food.

What could make them fly together like this?

Moonflower shielded her eyes and almost tripped over the grass as she watched the great flock pass overhead.

"What does this mean? Where are they going?" Bramble asked.

"I don't know," Moonflower said. "But they're going the same way we are—more or less. And look!" She pointed to a small flock of tiny birds that bobbed and darted around the back of the gathering of birds. They were bright red all over except for patches of black on their chests and faces.

"Are those goji berry birds?" Bramble gasped.

"Like Kigelia carried on his shoulder in the stories, showing him the way to the mountain. And it's not just that," she said, looking down and rubbing her eyes with her knuckles. "Mother told me that the Great Parent can control birds. I think this is a sign. We should follow them!"

"Well, we'd better get going then," said Bramble. Despite his thirst, he felt a new energy in his limbs. "They're going much faster than we are."

Sure enough, the two gorillas couldn't even begin to keep up with the birds in flight, and quite soon they had lost sight of them through the quavering haze. But Bramble tried not to let himself feel discouraged. They had a direction to head in, a little to the south of where they had been going. The birds might not have been sent to lead them, but they could still be a sign. In any case, usually birds lived in trees, and if there were trees, there must be water, right?

More and more, water was all Bramble could think about. His feet and knuckles raised little puffs of dust as they struck the dry earth, and he kept trying to swallow and then trying to suppress the cough that followed. Even the bristly tufts of grass seemed to be too dry to survive, as they emerged from the field onto an even flatter plain of brown earth and grass that lay flat to the ground, as if it was desperately trying to shelter from the burning heat of the sun.

Bramble's mind drifted to the crystal-clear streams of the

mountainside, some sparkling and cold from the far high peaks, others almost warm, running from the steaming vents of the Spirit Mouth. He imagined scooping up a handful of water and letting it run down his arms and splash on his toes, drinking deep, coolness running over his tongue . . . but he couldn't keep the fantasy going for more than a few seconds at a time. The reality of the heat and the soreness in his knuckles and feet from pounding the hard earth was too strong. His black fur seemed to soak up the sun, and when he reached up to scratch at his leathery face, it felt sore and hot to the touch.

Moonflower was obviously suffering too. She kept raising her knuckles to rub at her eyes, which Bramble was sure would only get more dust in them. Her gaze was fixed on the horizon, and her expression was almost angry, as if she wanted to draw it closer by sheer force of will.

If we don't find water soon, we won't make it, Bramble thought. The words rattled around his head, like a shriveled nut loose inside a shell. *We won't make it. Find water. Won't make it. Please, Great Spirit. Help us find water. . . .*

There *must* be water here somewhere, because still with every step he could see the quavering steam rising from the plain in front of him. Where could it be coming from?

And then he saw it. Something green, as green as the feathers on the bright birds, emerging from the swirling steam ahead of him. Spreading leaves over rippling water.

"Moonflower!" he said, his voice barely louder than a gasp. "Look! There's water!"

"Where?" Moonflower frowned. She squinted toward

where Bramble was pointing. "I don't . . . is that . . . ?"

A small voice in the back of Bramble's head said, *Can't she see it?* But he was already running, stumbling and tripping over his own feet in his hurry to get to the water. If he could just run a little faster, a little farther . . .

But the shining water wasn't growing any closer. He stumbled to a halt and blinked, horrified, as the green wavered and faded. The horizon seemed to swim and rearrange itself. The green leaves he'd seen were more birds, far away. The water was nothing but an empty, brown dip in the land that had seemed full up with that vanishing haze.

"No," he croaked. "Come on!" He dropped to his knees and then heavily onto his side, pounding the dry earth with one bruised fist. "Why would the Great Spirit do this?" he muttered.

He felt a hand on his elbow, pulling him up, and tried to shake it off. He didn't want Moonflower's sympathy. She would just say something sensible, and he wasn't in the mood. . . .

But it wasn't Moonflower. Bramble turned to look, squinting into the sunlight, and saw a larger gorilla peering back at him. His fur seemed to shimmer just like the surface of the water had done.

It was Cassava.

"Brother . . . ?" Bramble rasped.

"It's going to be okay," Cassava said. "Come here, little brother."

Bramble let Cassava help him upright. He couldn't seem

to focus on him properly, but the face was right, the voice was right. . . .

"You're dead," Bramble said. Cassava gripped his shoulders with both hands and lowered his head to rest against Bramble's. It felt cool, as if just for a moment, he had found water after all. Bramble closed his eyes.

"You know where you belong," Cassava's voice said. "One day you will be Silverback, and your troop needs you. You must turn back, Bramble. Turn around and go back to the mountain."

"But . . ." Bramble opened his eyes, and the face in front of his was not Cassava's at all.

"Are you all right?" Moonflower said. Her hands squeezed where they were holding his shoulders. "You called me Cassava! Are you seeing things?"

"He told me to turn back," Bramble said, pulling back and rubbing his eyes.

"What?"

"He said the troop needs me. That I should go back to the mountain."

Moonflower chewed thoughtfully on her fingernail for a moment. "I don't think you can trust these visions," she said at last. "We can't turn back now."

Bramble glared at her. "You said you saw Dayflower in the mist, and she led you the right way! What about that?"

"For a start, I'm the Mistback now," Moonflower said. "I'm *supposed* to see things. You're not. Plus, the water wasn't real, was it? And look." She turned and pointed back the way they'd come, and Bramble sighed. He almost hadn't realized they had walked so far, but the mountain was almost invisible now.

"We'll never make it," Moonflower said. "We'd die of thirst, or get eaten by lions, before we made it halfway back. We have to keep following the birds."

Bramble gave a groaning sigh. To his surprise, though his throat was still prickly and dry, it felt quite good to let it out.

Moonflower was right. That wasn't really Cassava, just like the shimmering water wasn't real. Cassava had died because of the evil on the mountain—he would want them to carry on, to get their message to the Great Parent.

"All right," he said. "Then let's go, before anything else weird happens."

The water, when they found it, was completely ordinary, warm and full of grit, and Bramble thought he might have never been happier to see something in his life.

There was no hint that the gully existed until they were right on top of it. The earth abruptly dropped into a deep and shady riverbed that threaded across the plain for as far as Bramble could see in both directions. It was almost completely dried up, but at the bottom a thin rivulet of brown water ran between little tufts of green grasses.

The gorillas splashed down to the stream and cupped the water in their hands. It felt so good, Bramble threw back two handfuls so fast it stung the back of his throat and he fell down coughing.

"Careful," Moonflower panted. "If you drink too much all at once, when you haven't had any all day, it'll be bad for your stomach. Little sips."

"Thanks, Mistback," Bramble said with a grin, scooping another handful of brown water. He drank more carefully and paused between scoops to catch his breath, looking up and down the gully in amazement.

It was running, which meant it must come from somewhere, but Bramble couldn't work out quite where—this wasn't like the mountain, where water always came from the higher slopes, running in little waterfalls from the rocks. There was no high ground for this water to come from. It seemed like it was emerging from the ground. There were holes in the wall of the riverbed that could have been some creature's home, or could have been vents to the deeper water, like at the Spirit Mouth.

"All right," Moonflower said finally. "I think we should go. We know this is here now, so if we don't make it to another pool by nightfall, we can come back."

"Okay." Bramble got up, feeling stiff. He wanted to suggest that they take a nap, but they had to keep moving if they were going to find the Great Parent in time to save the troop.

He bent to the deepest part of the water to scoop up one final mouthful, and his reflection blinked up at him.

But Bramble hadn't blinked.

"Go away, Cassava," Bramble muttered. "You were wrong about turning back. You're not real." He reached out to the water.

The reflection shattered, and Bramble snatched his hands away and threw himself backward just in time. Teeth snapped in the air right where his fingers had been, and a large, scaly head rose from the water. Bramble yelled for Moonflower and tried to scramble up the bank, but it was too steep, and too late. The lizard-thing lunged, mouth open, and clamped its teeth down hard on Bramble's leg. He clawed at the rocks to try to hold on but couldn't get purchase. The lizard was too strong. It dragged him, bleeding and screaming, into the water.

CHAPTER EIGHT

Prance walked toward the watering hole with her horns held high, trying to look calm, although inside she felt a rush of emotions buffeting her this way and that like the winds battering a lone tree in a storm. One moment she was enjoying a sense of pride and excitement to be arriving at her first Great Gathering with the Great Father's own entourage, the next she was struck by a fleeting burst of deep ancestral terror at walking beside Gallant, and then she spotted the watering hole in the distance and was filled with awe, and nervousness too.

There were so many creatures there already. She couldn't make many of them out from this distance, but the crowd was big enough that it stood out against the pale morning grass and the shining surface of the water. She could tell that there were giraffes and elephants, and birds circling above, but the crowd was so big, so varied and constantly moving, it almost seemed like one huge, breathing animal.

"Good morning, Great Father!" chirped a voice, and Prance looked down to see a small colony of mongoose racing past, ten lithe, striped brown bodies looking like ripples in the grass as they ran.

"Good morning, Snap," Thorn said, with a wave.

Prance looked back toward Moth, who was bringing up the rear with Mud. She was thinking about asking how many Gatherings Moth had been to, or just how many creatures there would be, but Moth and Mud looked like they were deep in conversation.

"I'm just saying, it felt like a good thing to me," Moth said.

"You mean it felt *satisfying*," Mud corrected her. "I know it can be confusing. Believe me, I remember my early stone-readings. It was exciting, knowing that I could see things in them others couldn't, even if what they told me was frightening."

"Well, that too," Moth admitted.

"It was a good reading," Mud told her, obviously trying to sound reassuring. "Thorn will send a vulture to see if anything comes of it, or any creatures need to be warned. An avalanche in the mountains can be a dangerous thing."

"Good. But . . ." Moth frowned at a pebble in front of her and kicked it out of the way. "But even so, I just have this *feeling* that it wasn't as simple as that. *Two black boulders, rolling down from the mountain . . .* What if it's not an avalanche?"

"It's completely normal to second-guess stone-readings," Mud said. "Especially when you don't want to believe what you've seen. Trust me."

Prance didn't say anything, but she could see both Mud's and Moth's points of view. It was hard when the Great Spirit seemed to be giving you a message you didn't understand. She looked down at the bright grass beneath her, where her shadow should have been, and wondered what the animals at the Gathering would think. Most of them wouldn't know what it meant to lose the Us or be chosen for death, but surely they would know there was something wrong. . . .

Before they reached the edge of the water, Prance felt a tremor in the ground and looked up, her heart in her mouth, to see a small group of elephants trotting across the plain to meet them. The largest matriarch led the way, lifting her enormous feet and tossing her trunk in greeting. Prance saw the Great Father's expression change, and he straightened up and started to hop toward the elephant, his aches and pains forgotten, at least for the moment.

He looks like a young baboon, Prance thought.

The elephant stopped, with great care, before the Great Father, looming over him with an expression of joy. Thorn put his arms up and held her trunk for a moment, before letting it go.

"Sky," he said. "It has been a long time! The herd is back?" He leaned to try to look around the elephant, though the best he could do was peer through her legs.

"We're back," said Sky.

Mud hurried past Prance to greet Sky too, and she reached out her trunk to gently touch the top of his head. He let out an unguarded laugh, for the first time since Prance had met him.

Prance watched this reunion in awe and disbelief.

It's Sky!

The third of the three heroes, the elephant who carried the Great Spirit when it had nowhere else to go—granddaughter of the last true Great Mother, matriarch of the herd that took in zebras and rhinos and cheetah cubs, defeater of tyrants. She was here, standing in front of Prance, fussing Mud's fur as if she was just any old elephant.

Prance couldn't help wondering if the two heroes missed their friend Fearless. He'd given his life to save Bravelands. What must it be like to be left behind?

"How are your calves? Are they here?" Thorn asked, still trying to look behind Sky.

"Dawn is here," Sky said, and Prance saw a younger female elephant step around Sky, blinking shyly. "Typhoon left to be with the bulls at the end of the winter."

"Already? They grow up so fast." Thorn shook his head.

Sky sighed. "Well, he wanted to take his place with his uncles, after . . . we lost his father last season."

"Oh, I'm sorry." Thorn reached up and placed his wrinkled hands against the thick skin of Sky's foreleg. "Rock's with his ancestors now, roaming the plain of stars."

Sky smiled sadly. "And making all sorts of trouble, I'm sure."

Thorn chuckled.

"Would you like a lift, Great Father?" Sky asked.

"I would love one," Thorn said.

Dawn, the younger elephant, knelt down and bent her head

so that Thorn could easily climb up her trunk and perch on her shoulders, and the elephants turned and led them to the edge of the watering hole. Prance followed them, still in awe.

"Come and stand with me," Moth said and led her to a spot on the bank beside a large rock that stuck out over the water.

As they approached the crowd, Sky raised her trunk and let out a great trumpet, and every animal at the Gathering fell silent as Thorn slid down from Dawn's back and stepped out onto the rock. Mud scrambled up to sit behind him, and Gallant lay down at the base of the rock, with his paws neatly together in front of him. Prance got a strong impression that he was pretending to be relaxed but was actually watching the crowd carefully.

"My fellow creatures," Thorn said, and his voice carried over the stillness of the water, surprisingly strong and clear from the elderly baboon's throat. "Greetings, and thank you for coming. I have called this Gathering to give a warning, and to reassure you. I have heard many strange stories in the last few days. And there were more, I think, that I could not hear."

Prance saw him give a nod to his left, and she looked over the water to see the elderly hyena he'd had to turn away. She let out a snort but didn't interrupt.

"I know some of the things that have been happening lately are upsetting and confusing," Thorn went on. "But Bravelands has faced challenges before and overcome them. If there is a new storm on the horizon, make no mistake, we will weather it together. Who can forget the reign of the false

Great Parents, or Titan and his pack of wolves?"

Prance saw many of the creatures nodding, especially the longer-lived ones—the elephants, a spurred tortoise, some of the colorful birds. But others exchanged knowing glances or sniffed disdainfully.

"That was the distant past," said an older monkey. "You're not the young baboon you were then."

"And who knows if the stories are even true," said another, who Prance thought was probably like her, too young to remember the time of the wolves. "Whoever heard of spirit-eating lions?"

"It's true," rumbled Sky. "We lived through it. Listen to your elders, young monkey."

The older monkey elbowed her younger companion, and the younger one looked a little bit sheepish.

"But these problems aren't like Titan, are they?" said a zebra nervously. "It's not as if there's a wolf pack roaming Bravelands. Things are just . . . *weird*." There was a chorus of agreement from the creatures around him.

"My foal is still missing!"

"Strange noises in the walls of our burrow . . ."

"The starlings have never been aggressive before. . . ."

The zebra lifted his head and spoke more boldly. "The Great Spirit must be displeased with us! There's nothing else to link these problems."

The water stirred, and Prance jumped as she realized that what she'd taken for a large rock in the watering hole was actually the basking back of a hippopotamus. The hippo rose out of the water, snorting.

"Maybe the Great Spirit is sickening," he declared. "Maybe Bravelands is suffering because the Spirit has spent too long in the same weak body. The Great Father can hardly see, let alone fight some mysterious *wrongness* spreading across the plains. Maybe it's time for a stronger, more powerful leader."

Prance looked up at Thorn, feeling stung and anxious on his behalf. But Thorn's eyes narrowed.

"Such as a hippo?" he said.

A ripple of laughter passed through the crowd, and the hippo snorted and sank back into the water.

"Perhaps," he muttered.

"My friends, listen," Thorn said. "I know I am old. But my spirit is strong, and the Great Spirit is strong within me. But more importantly, our strength has always been in our unity. We must help each other, now more than ever. Be vigilant, and talk to one another. Know that I will always be watching, and we will find out what links these strange occurrences. If you see anything untoward, you can always come to me."

"There's *something untoward* standing right beside you," said a familiar, tremulous voice.

Prance looked out over the water and felt her heart miss a beat as she saw a group of gazelles move to the front of the crowd. The one who had spoken was Fleet Runningherd. Over her shoulder Prance could see Bolt and Fly, and behind them, Skip. Her best friend. She shuddered as Skip awkwardly avoided her gaze, remembering her awful dream.

"That gazelle," Fleet said, "is Prance Herdless, and she is

marked for death. Look—she has no shadow!"

Prance felt the weight of every animal's gaze on her and shifted her hooves nervously in the scrubby grass. But she made herself lock eyes with Fleet. If she was going to be accused of something, she wanted to make her accuser look her in the eye.

"Fleet Runningherd," said Thorn, his voice calm and curious. "Please tell us, for those who don't know the ways of the gazelle. What does it mean when a gazelle loses their shadow but does not die?"

"I . . . I don't know," Fleet said. "She lost the Us. She was supposed to die. This has never happened before!"

"Exactly," said Thorn. "You don't know for what purpose Prance was spared death, and nor do I. It seems to me that the Great Spirit has intervened, and that is not for us to question."

Prance felt a flush of pride, and a little embarrassment, creeping under her hide. She steeled herself for Fleet's reaction, still keeping her eyes on the gazelles, but it wasn't Fleet who replied—it was Skip.

Prance's best friend stepped forward. "Great Father is right," she said. "I—our whole herd—condemned Prance for what happened to her. But we've been talking about it ever since, and I think the Great Spirit saved Prance for a reason. It may be unnatural, but it is *not* untoward. And I think we should welcome Prance back into the herd."

Skip looked over the water at Prance and gave her a small, hopeful smile that made Prance's heart swell.

"And I agree with Skip," said Bolt. "The Us misses you, Prance. We all do."

One by one, each of the gazelles nodded and stamped their hooves in agreement, apart from Fleet, who stared at the ground. Prance's ears twitched as she turned to Thorn, feeling excited and nervous and . . . deep down, strangely, a little doubtful.

"Great Father, can I speak to you?" she said under her breath, and Thorn seemed to understand at once. He held up his hand to the braying gazelles and turned away from the gathering, sitting down on the edge of the rock so he could lean his head close to Prance's. "What should I do?" she asked him.

"Well, I can't tell you that," said Thorn. "All I can tell you is that you must look into your heart. It will tell you where you need to be."

Prance nodded, and even though she could still feel the gaze of every creature at the Gathering on her, she closed her eyes and tried to look into her heart. She imagined herself returning to her family, Prance Runningherd once again . . . leaving Thorn with the problems of Bravelands . . . leaving Moth . . . She imagined herself journeying with the herd, and it was wonderful to be back among friends . . . but there was still something missing.

She opened her eyes and looked across the water to the herd.

"Skip—all of you—I'm so grateful. Thank you. And one

day, I know I'll be able to come back to the herd. . . . But not yet."

Skip's dark eyes went wide, and Prance tried to smile a little at her.

I want to come home, she thought. *But I can't—please, I hope you understand. . . .*

"I don't have the Us," Prance went on. "If I were to come back now, I'd always be out of place. I think the Great Father is right, and this is happening to me for a reason. Until I find out what that is, I can't return to the herd."

"We understand," Skip said quietly. "The herd wishes you well. We hope you find what you're looking for soon." She bowed her head, and Prance bowed back. It hurt her heart to be so close to them, but she knew the watering hole that separated them might as well have been as wide as the plains.

"My friends, the time has come to end our Gathering," said Thorn, getting up with a small grunt of effort. "I thank you all for coming, and I promise you, I may be an old baboon, but I will get to the bottom of these strange occurrences. Farewell, and may the Great Spirit watch over you all."

Some of the animals cried out their farewells and good wishes to Thorn as he turned to let Sky help him down from the jutting rock, but Prance saw some of them simply standing around, talking to the herd-mates they'd come with in low voices. She sensed an unfinished, unsettled feeling around the watering hole, and she was sure Thorn could probably sense it too.

But he'll find the answers, she thought. *I believe in him—and I'll be helping him, too.*

Dawn and Sky walked with them back as far as the edge of the forest, the Great Father riding on Dawn's shoulders once again, with Prance, Gallant, Moth, and Mud walking behind. Before the elephants left, Sky wrapped her trunk gently around Thorn.

"I hope we'll see you again soon," she said. "Take care of yourself, Thorn."

Thorn patted Sky's trunk as she unwound it, and he and Mud both waved as the two elephants walked back to their herd, their long unhurried strides still moving faster than the baboons could have done at a flat run.

As they walked through the trees to the Great Father's clearing, Prance found herself walking ahead of Thorn and Mud, with Moth beside her.

"It was brave of you not to go back," Moth said. Prance smiled slightly.

"I'm not sure it was brave. I just knew I couldn't. I think I need to be here. And anyway, I want to help Great Father." She took a deep breath. "I was thinking of volunteering to go visit some of the animals who he couldn't get to. I can move fast, and if Gallant comes with me I'll be safe. What do you think—do you think he'd like that?"

"Sounds like a great idea!" Moth said. "We can ask Thorn after he's had his nap."

"Of course." Prance chuckled. "Nothing can interrupt the Great . . ."

She stopped.

Something was wrong.

For a moment, she almost thought the Us had returned. This feeling was similar, a deep twinge of unease in her gut, just like she would feel when the Us sensed danger approaching the herd. It wasn't the Us—she still felt that strange and disquieting sense of being alone—but now she knew, somehow, that the grass ahead was full of dangers. Her vision seemed to swim and sharpen, and then she saw the movement, the shadows swimming through the grass.

"Snakes!" she yelled, rearing up. "Look out!"

There were dozens of them. Black and glossy cobras, which reared up at her shout, hissing and spreading their necks as if they were yelling back in defiance. Mottled puff adders, long fangs dripping with venom, and black mambas with their deathly gray bellies. Watching the snakes swarm up to the Great Parent's entourage, Prance felt as if she was living through the cautionary tale the elders of the herd told their foals to warn them to be careful where they put their hooves in the long grass.

But she knew what to do.

She raised her hooves and let out a shriek of fear as she struck down hard at the first snake that came within her reach. Even as she felt a sickening crunch and the snake stopped moving, more were swarming past her.

"Grab behind their heads!" Moth yelled. "So they can't— eek!"

She ducked as a black-necked cobra spat its venom at her.

It flew over her head, missing her by a hair. Prance put her head down and used her horns to toss the cobra up out of the grass and send it spinning away. As she turned back, one of the adders lashed out and tried to bite into her ankle, but she reared up and smashed her hooves down on it instead.

This is like a nightmare, she thought as she looked back. Moth was wrestling with another snapping adder, and Gallant was tearing one of the cobras to pieces. Mud picked up a nearby rock and threw it, smacking one of the snakes across the back of the head. Dead or stunned, it lay still in the grass.

Then Thorn screamed with pain, and all of them turned at once. Clinging to his arm, its venom-ridden fangs drawing scratches across his fur as he pushed it away, was a black mamba.

CHAPTER NINE

"You shouldn't have brought him here," Seek growled again.

Chase let out a small grunt of frustration and batted at the cub with her paw, moving him away from the mouth of the den where Shadow was resting. Perhaps it was good he had slipped into a feverish sleep, semiconscious and twitching— she was worried for the black leopard, but right now, she was even more angry with Seek.

"How could you say that?" she said.

"I'm just being practical," Seek snarled back. "We should move on. Abandon him. He's weak; he'll probably die in there."

"You're being *horrible*," Chase said. She looked up at the tree above them, searching the branches for snakes. She didn't want to be out here, but she couldn't have this conversation with Seek inside, where Shadow would hear them. It'd break his heart. "Shadow cared for you when I couldn't. He's our friend."

"You didn't seem like you thought he was a friend when you came to steal me back." Seek sat back on his haunches, his fluffy tail thumping irritably against the ground. "It was you who led those hyenas to him and then left him all alone. You're a hypocrite!"

"I know," said Chase miserably. "It's my fault he got hurt—but I realized I was wrong, and I'm trying to make up for it. Why can't you understand that?"

"What happened to *Trust only yourself*?" Seek spat.

Chase reeled back. "Don't repeat my own mother's words back to me!"

"Well, if she was here she'd agree with me," said Seek. "She'd say you were being a fool. Shadow can't even hunt—what use is he to us? He's no good as a mate, if that's what you were thinking. He's just another mouth to feed."

"What? I wasn't . . ." Chase stared at Seek, her heart pounding. "I didn't say anything about a *mate*. What's gotten into you?"

Seek was just a cub, cheeks fluffy, even though he was growing every day. Chase still loomed over him. So why did it seem as if he had gone to sleep as a sweet, innocent cub and woken up with the heart of a grown, bitter leopard?

Seek ignored her question. His eyes bored into hers, and they still looked bloodshot, almost a whole day after he'd been bitten.

"If you wanted a male to drag home and live happily ever

after, you should have stuck with Range," he said. "He was strong. He had territory."

"His territory was infested with snakes!" Chase yowled before she caught herself. What was she saying? What was *Seek* saying? "They *bit* you, Seek! You almost died, and Range was behind it! Don't you remember?" She searched his face, but his expression didn't change. He still stared at her with baleful, angry eyes, his lip curled in something like contempt. It frightened Chase, almost more than the snake attack had.

"Chase?" said a weak voice from the mouth of the den. Shadow emerged from the darkness, walking on all four paws, but so low to the ground it was almost a crawl. His head hung low and his eyes looked red. "I need water."

Chase sighed and looked from Shadow's gently swaying form to Seek, who was bristling, as if Shadow's weakness offended him. She couldn't let Shadow go to the river alone in his state, but she couldn't leave Seek either.

"We'll all go," she said. "It'll be safer that way."

Although if they all went down to the river together, in the daylight, there was nothing to stop Range finding them there. Would she be able to protect them both?

She had no choice; she had to risk it, but the question gnawed at her as they made their way cautiously across the mountainside and down to the edge of the river. She slowly circled the others, scouting ahead and then hanging back to make sure they weren't being followed.

The river was deserted, aside from a few brightly colored birds who took to the sky as the leopards approached. Chase held the others back, sniffing carefully along the bank and listening intently for danger. But then she stepped back and let Shadow pass her to the edge of the water. Seek drank too, but Chase waited, flicking her gaze from the tree branches to the bushes on the opposite side of the river.

Shadow drank for a long time, lapping at the cool rushing river. When he looked up, licking his lips, Chase was pleased to see his eyes were a little brighter, and he sat back on his haunches and started to clean his face.

Then something moved on the opposite bank, and Chase sat bolt upright and then nudged her way in front of Seek and Shadow, standing with her front paws in the water to put herself between them and whatever was in the bushes.

The leaves stirred, and then Chase caught the scent.

Hyena.

"Get back," she told the others as the brown striped creature pushed through the bushes.

It was the same hyena she had seen before, the one who had been too injured to move. She looked up, saw Chase, and froze. Chase tensed to turn and run, in case more hyenas were right behind her. But the hyena chuckled to herself and bent her head to drink, and Chase realized she was alone.

"Thank you for the prey," the hyena said between mouthfuls of water. "I feel much stronger now."

"What's she talking about?" Seek snarled.

"Nothing," muttered Chase.

"*You*," said Shadow. He stepped up to stand beside Chase, and though she wished he would let her handle this, at least he seemed a little stronger. "I thought I'd killed you!"

"Feeling's mutual," said the hyena. "But I see you made it, after all. You and your concerned friend here."

"No thanks to you," Chase snapped. "You told the other hyenas where we were!"

"Of course I did," the hyena said. "I'm no leopard. I bought my life from them just like I bought it from you."

"Enough!" A high-pitched roar came from behind Chase, and before she could react Seek had waded into the water, up to his chest, and was yowling at the hyena. "If you want a fight, I'll give you a fight! I'll take you on all by myself!"

The hyena gave Seek an intense stare and the bristling fur on her back stood up on end. She was smaller than a grown leopard, but still more than twice as big as Seek.

"Try it, cub," she said. "If you can cross the river without being washed away . . ."

"Seek, no!" Chase reached over and seized him by the scruff and pulled him back out of the water. "What are you doing, you'll be—ow!" she yelped as Seek turned around and bit her on the leg.

"I know what I'm doing!" Seek snarled.

Before Chase could reply, she heard a chuckling sound start up across the river. The hyena was laughing at them.

"Shut up!" Seek snapped at her.

"Oh," the hyena giggled, "this is too good. Let me guess, the cub's been bitten? By a snake?"

Chase shivered. She felt as if the cool river water had frozen around her paws. "How did you know?"

The hyena peered around Chase to look at Seek, a smile creeping across her face. "He has the madness in his eyes," she said.

"I'm not mad!" Seek yowled and made a dash for the edge of the river again. Chase snapped for his scruff and missed, but Shadow caught him by the tail and pulled him back, writhing and screaming curses at both of them.

"That is no longer the cub you knew," said the hyena. "He is already lost. He just doesn't know it yet."

Chase watched as Shadow managed to wrestle Seek back, and Seek sat down, glaring across the river with bloodshot eyes. She thought of the way he'd turned against Shadow, the way he'd woken up and rejected her. . . .

But this couldn't be right.

"It can't be the snakebite," she said, turning back to the hyena. She held up her own paw and showed off the pale break in the fur. "I'm not mad, and I was bitten too."

"And when was the last time you ate rot-meat?" the hyena asked.

"*Never*," Chase retorted, pulling a face. "I don't—"

But she had. The image of the monkey, flies swarming around its rotting body, swam in front of her eyes. She'd been desperate and starving. She'd needed the energy to hunt something fresh for Seek. She hadn't let him eat the rot-meat. . . .

"I did. A few days ago," she admitted.

"Then you should find some more," said the hyena. "And

your friend too, before he treads on the wrong snake and turns, just like your cub. The rot-meat will keep you safe from the curse."

"You're the one who's mad," Shadow snarled, "if you think we're going to believe any of this. Come on, Chase. She's trying to trick us into eating rot-meat so we get sick and die. You can't be seriously considering it."

"Right . . . ," Chase said, but she didn't feel at all sure.

The hyena shrugged. "Believe what you want. Hyenas eat rot-meat all the time. It makes you sick, but then it makes you *strong*. We can eat anything we choose, and we shake off the snake's curse. Wait a while. You'll see what happens if you don't protect yourselves."

Chase turned to look back at Seek, a dizzy feeling of anxiety in her gut—but Seek wasn't there.

"Seek?" she said. She sniffed the air ground where she'd last seen him and caught his trail leading off into the bushes. "Seek!"

"I told you," said the hyena. "The cub has the sickness. His mind is not his own."

Chase couldn't waste any more time. Seek couldn't have gone too far, but if she didn't follow him now . . .

"Chase, wait!" Shadow said behind her, as she leaped over a bush and pressed into the undergrowth.

The hyena's right, she thought, as she ran. *Seek's not in his right mind, and it's all my fault.*

CHAPTER TEN

Bramble writhed and clawed at the muddy stream bed. He felt the water close over his head, hot and muddy, as the lizard's jaws clamped down on his leg and it dragged him down toward one of the holes in the bank. Bramble flailed, his fingers caught rock, and he managed to wrestle himself upright, his head bursting from the surface of the water. He coughed and spat out a mouthful of grit, and without waiting to wipe his eyes, he balled his fist and aimed a thump at the place on his leg where the pain was throbbing. It struck something fleshy with a satisfying *thump*, and the pressure loosened. Bramble got up and limped away, splashing through the stream and throwing himself up the near-vertical bank to Moonflower's side.

"What happened?" Moonflower gasped, helping him up and peering over the edge.

"Keep back!" Bramble grabbed Moonflower's shoulder and

half fell away from the stream, pulling her with him. Then he raised his hands and scrubbed at his face, finally clearing his vision.

"Bramble, your leg!" Moonflower said. She bent to examine it, as a Mistback would, as she'd learned from Dayflower.

"Something grabbed me," Bramble yelped. "Some kind of—look out!"

Over Moonflower's shoulder, the creature burst from the gully, slapping its clawed feet down on the top of the bank, its forked tongue flicking out to taste the air. Moonflower looked around, gasped, and jumped right over Bramble's legs to get behind him, tuck her hands into his armpits, and pull him away from the edge.

Which left Bramble with a clear, unobstructed view of the creature as it hissed at him. The scales on its head were a faded black-brown, and Bramble could see that its arms and back were striped with scales of dirty pale cream. It turned its head this way and that, and he realized its eyes were white and filmy. It was blind. But it still searched for him, sniffing with its tongue for his scent.

He managed to get up and back away, Moonflower still holding on to his shoulders. The lizard opened its jaws and hissed once more, and then, thank the Great Spirit, it slowly lowered itself back over the edge of the gully and disappeared.

Bramble and Moonflower exchanged terrified looks and backed farther away from the gully, until Bramble found a rock to sit down on and Moonflower could look closer at his leg. She prodded the place where the lizard's jaws had closed.

Black bruises were swelling up, visible even under his dark fur, and her touch made Bramble wince.

"Where did it come from?" she whispered, glancing over her shoulder.

"Under the water, I think?" Bramble groaned. "There must have been a cave, or a tunnel, or—ow!—or something."

Moonflower slowly examined all around his leg.

"It's all right," she said. "It's not bleeding. Stand up?"

Bramble did. The leg didn't like it at all—it hurt—but he could take his own weight.

He stared back at the gully, his racing heart starting to slow.

"Attacked by a sandtongue," he said. He gave Moonflower a meaningful look. "Don't you think that's strange, after everything that's happening at home?"

"You think it's . . . connected somehow?" Moonflower looked back at him as if he'd gone mad, then seemed to think it through and shook her head. "No, it has to be a coincidence. We're so far from the mountain! We were just unlucky. We'll be more careful next time."

Bramble sighed. "I hope you're right."

They had to cross the gully to keep moving in the direction they'd seen the birds flying, but they walked to a place where the banks were shallower and less steep first, and Bramble kept a keen, anxious eye on the water the whole time. When they'd made it to the other side, they both started to walk faster, though Bramble's leg still ached, coming to an unspoken agreement that it would be good to put some distance between them and the blind lizard.

The sun finally started to slip toward the horizon, and Bramble stopped to shade his eyes and look ahead. The sunset was as spectacular on the plains as the sunrise had been, without the looming trunks of trees or the mountain slopes to get in the way. The sky turned red, the clouds glowing bright orange.

"I see some trees," he said, peering in the direction they were moving. "Not many, but at least it'll be somewhere to shelter for the night."

"And they're really there this time," Moonflower added. "Come on, let's go!"

The copse was a group of six trees, each like the one where they'd sheltered from the stampede, but a little taller and with greener leaves. Bramble and Moonflower swung cautiously up into the branches, checking for more strange creatures that might wish them harm, and then curled up side by side against the trunk.

The red sky had turned to deep blue and then to black, and the ground below was shrouded in darkness. Bramble tried to close his eyes and fall asleep, but his heart was racing. He jumped as a strange yowling cry echoed across the plains, and then another answered it from far away. Insects hummed in the grass around the tree. There were scuffling noises from below, something that Bramble thought sounded like claws raking wood. A squeaking cry that cut off suddenly.

Bramble looked up, trying to ignore the nightmarish nocturnal business of the plains. He peered through the leaves of the tree at the stars and felt a little bit calmed. It was just as if he'd been back at home, sitting in the tall branches of the mountain trees.

Then a shape passed across the stars. It moved in a banking circular pattern, closer and closer to the branch. Bramble made out a large wingspan and a long, curved neck. It was a vulture.

In a moment it had swooped down and landed on a branch up above Bramble's head.

"Go away!" he hissed. "There's nothing for you here! Go on, shoo!"

The vulture peered down at him for a long, unsettling second. Then it took off again, wheeling away into the sky and vanishing into the darkness. Bramble closed his eyes and put his arms over his head, trying not to think about where it might be going next.

He didn't remember falling asleep, but Bramble jolted awake with a start to find bright, pale sunshine streaming through the leaves, and a thick, gray snake grasping for him through the branches.

He let out a shriek and scrambled back, clumsily trying to shake Moonflower awake and hop to the next branch at the same time. Moonflower awoke with a yell and looked around, panic and confusion in her eyes. Behind her, the snake slipped away and was gone.

"Snake!" Bramble yelped, pointing to where it had been. "Get away, over here!"

Moonflower almost fell from the branch in her hurry to

clamber over to the branch beside him, and then looked in the direction he was pointing, rubbing her eyes.

"Bramble, there's nothing there!" she groaned. "You were dreaming."

"It's hiding!" Bramble hissed. He looked around at the branches, terrified that he'd see more of the strange, wrinkled gray snakes swarming all around them. But there was nothing.

"It's understandable that you might be seeing things," Moonflower said, yawning. "After what happened yester—"

She broke off with a yelp as the whole tree seemed to suddenly shake. Branches bent and bowed, and the leaves moved as if in a strong wind.

"Am I seeing things now?" Bramble gasped.

The branch underneath them swayed, and Moonflower reached out to steady herself, but she grabbed a thin branch that snapped in her grip, her foot slipped, and with a yelp she was gone, falling through the leaves.

"Moonflower!" Bramble cried and swung after her, hopping from branch to branch and sliding down the tree trunk until he came to a thumping halt on the ground. He spun around, expecting to see Moonflower either on the empty plain or fighting off a writhing snake, but instead he found a great expanse of gray, leathery hide blocking his view. He jumped and backed up against the tree, trying to understand what he was looking at.

Moonflower had fallen into the midst of a group of creatures—*huge* ones, more than twice as big as the wildebeest. They had massive gray bodies, thin tails with short brushes, and ears as big as a gorilla. Through their legs, which were like tree trunks, he could make out Moonflower getting up from the floor, not badly hurt, but trembling with shock.

Bramble took a deep breath. If Moonflower was going to die, he wouldn't let her die alone. He stood up, pounded his chest, and let out the loudest roar he could muster.

The closest creature to him jumped, which in itself was terrifying enough to cut Bramble's roar off with a squeaky yelp. The creature lumbered around, its huge flat feet kicking up mud and grass, and raised the thing that must be its nose, the thing Bramble had mistaken for a snake. It made a long blaring noise, like nothing Bramble had ever heard before, and he saw its two giant tusks and, inside its mouth, teeth longer than his arm.

He grabbed a broken branch from the roots of the tree and held it in front of him, but the beast's nose-thing reached out and grabbed the stick, just like a hand would, and pulled it up into the air. Bramble tugged back, but he was no match for the strength of the creature and found himself dangling in mid-air, hooting with fear.

"What are you?" said the creature.

Bramble looked down and caught a glimpse of Moonflower, backing away from more of the creatures. None of them were actually trying to stomp her, but if they decided to, she would be little more than a smear in the pale grass.

"We're gorillas, and I won't let you hurt my friend!" Bramble yelled. He tried to take one hand off the branch and swipe at the animal, but he couldn't reach.

The creature's eyes narrowed in confusion, but behind her, several of the other giants burst into laughter.

"That's a good one," said one of them.

"Everyone knows there's no such thing as gorillas," said another, smaller one, who walked up close beside the one holding Bramble. "What are you really? Some kind of monkey?"

Bramble was startled into silence. *No such thing as gorillas?*

"Well, what are *you*?" Moonflower said. "Overgrown mice?"

The massive creature slowly lowered her long nose, and Bramble found himself being gently put back down on the ground.

"We're elephants. And we won't hurt either of you," she said. Her voice was surprisingly quiet for such an enormous animal. "My name is Sky. This is Dawn, and this is our herd."

Bramble gingerly put down the branch. Moonflower cautiously backed out of the circle of elephants to his side. Sky blinked large, gentle eyes at the two of them.

"Do you have a troop?" she asked. "We don't often see . . . creatures like you in isolated trees like this, out in the middle of the plains."

"We don't see creatures like you at all," said Dawn. "Are you *really* gorillas?"

"Yes," said Moonflower. "Our troop lives on the mountain."

"Mother?" Dawn said, giving Sky an awestruck look.

Sky dipped her head to look closely at the two gorillas. "I think they must be," she said. "The stories say that your ancestors vanished from Bravelands, long ago. What are you doing down here on the plains?"

"We're looking for the Great Parent," Bramble said. "Do you know where they are?"

"Yes, he's over that way!" Dawn said, pointing with her long nose. "We just came from a Great Gathering."

"Why are you looking for Thorn?" Sky asked. "Did something happen?"

Bramble and Moonflower looked at each other. Bramble wasn't sure why, because these elephants seemed friendly enough, but he suddenly felt like he didn't want to tell them too much about the troop's problems.

"There's just . . . some strange things happening on the mountain," he said.

Sky hesitated for a moment, then nodded. "I understand. There are strange things happening all over Bravelands, it seems. You had better find the Great Father quickly. You see that kopje, there?"

She pointed with her nose in the same direction as the smaller elephant, and Bramble squinted at the horizon. He made out what she was pointing at—it was a hill, standing up in the middle of a flat plain, with what looked like a tree and a few rocks springing up from it.

"When you pass it, you'll see the edge of the forest. Great Father Thorn's clearing is just beyond the tree line. You can ask any creature you meet in the forest if you need more directions."

"Thank you!" said Moonflower. "Um, I'm sorry if this

is a silly question, but . . . what kind of creature is the Great Father?"

Sky laughed, and a few of the other elephants twitched their ears in amusement.

"Whatever you are, you're certainly not from the plains," one of them snorted.

"He's a baboon," Sky said. "Do you know what that is?"

"It's a kind of monkey," said Moonflower, a note of awe in her voice. "My mother told me about them. That means he's a bit like us!"

"That's right," said Sky. "You had better get going. You'll make it by nightfall if you hurry."

"Thank you so much," Bramble said. "Our troop will remember your help."

Sky blinked happily and stepped back, nudging Dawn to follow her and give the gorillas room.

Bramble looked back as they started to walk away and waved an arm when he saw Sky watching them go. The rest of the elephants were gathered around the tree, pulling the leaves down with their long, grabby noses.

Perhaps the plains weren't *so* terrifying. If such giant creatures were plant-eaters, and the Great Father was just like them, perhaps there was more to the plains than spilled blood after all.

CHAPTER ELEVEN

Gallant seized the snake in his jaws and tore it from the Great Father's arm, biting down hard and then tossing his head to throw the snake hard against a tree, where it slipped down and lay still.

"Great Father!" Prance cried, rushing over to Thorn's side. The few snakes that hadn't already been killed seemed to melt away into the grass as she passed them. Mud and Moth hurried to him too, as he stumbled and steadied himself against the trunk of a tree. Gallant paced around them, radiating cold fury.

"Thorn, are you all right?" Mud asked.

"Just a scratch," Thorn said. "I'm . . . I'm fine. . . ." But as he said it, his eyes rolled and he gripped on to the tree, as if the ground had tipped underneath him. Moth put her shoulder under his and held him up, and Mud put his hands on the sides of Thorn's face and turned it so he could look into Thorn's eyes.

"Thorn? Thorn!"

"I'm here," Thorn said, but his voice was so weak and quiet, Prance could barely make it out.

"We need to get him to Grub Goodleaf at once," Mud said, his own voice trembling a little.

"I'll go get him," Prance said. "I can make it there and back faster than we can get Thorn there."

"Thank you!" Moth said. "The baboon troop lives just beyond the Great Father's clearing."

Mud turned and looked at Prance, a desolate, angry look in his eyes that startled her. But then he nodded.

"Run like the wind," he muttered. "Gallant, go with her."

Prance turned, kicking up leaves, and broke into a sprint. She hadn't moved this fast in days. No need for the Us now— terror for Thorn filled her with the same pounding fear. She ran in time with her racing heart, trusting to instinct as she sprang over bushes and dodged around trees. She heard Gallant's big paws thudding on the ground behind her, gradually fainter as she outpaced him. She crossed the Great Father's clearing in a heartbeat, barely registering the burst of sunshine on her back, and pressed deeper into the forest. She was aware of other creatures watching as she passed, flashes of color as birds took off from the trees, eyes staring from the shadows, but she had to concentrate as the ground grew rougher and the trees thicker. She clattered over rocks and tree roots and splashed through a river, until she started to see baboons in the trees.

At last, she burst into the clearing where the baboon troop was sitting. Several of them scattered, hooting in surprise and then confusion to see a gazelle standing there, sweat-beaded and gasping for breath.

"Grub Goodleaf?" she called between gulps of air. "I need to find the Goodleaf!"

"What's wrong?" said a large female baboon, stepping forward. Two baby baboons clung to her fur and blinked up at Prance with eyes that looked too big for their heads. "I'm Cashew Crownleaf, the leader of this troop. Why does a gazelle need to find our Goodleaf?"

"It's for the Great Father," Prance said. She pawed the ground with one hoof, searching the faces of the baboons, as if she could tell which one was Grub just by looking. "He's . . ."

"He's hurt his foot," said a rasping voice, and Gallant pushed through the undergrowth. His sides were heaving with the effort of keeping up with her. "Stood on a sharp stone. It's *no real danger*," he added.

He glared at Prance, and she twitched and looked away.

Of course, he doesn't want to tell everyone how bad it is. . . .

"That's right," she said. "It's not serious, but . . . it hurts, and he needs a Goodleaf right away."

"Here I am," said a baboon, swinging down from the branch of a tree. "Lead the way."

Prance turned and led Grub out of the baboon camp, trying

to look casual, matching Gallant's pace, for what felt like a painfully long time. Then Gallant paused, looked around, and nodded at Prance.

"Climb onto Prance's back," he said to Grub. "Hurry."

Grub gave them both a confused look but didn't ask any questions. Prance waited until he was firmly on her back and hanging on to her horns, then she nodded back at Gallant and took off again. It was strange, running with a baboon on her back, but she could go almost as fast, and to Grub's credit he managed to hang on and yelped only a couple of times, when she leaped over particularly large fallen logs.

"He hasn't really hurt his foot, has he?" Grub muttered into Prance's ear as they ran.

"No," Prance said.

They made it back to the part of the forest where she'd left Thorn, and Prance slowed to a halt and let Grub slide from her back. He hurried, a little unsteadily, over to the tree and bent down. Prance watched, her heart in her throat.

The Great Father was lying on the ground, on what looked like a bed made of leaves. Mud and Moth were both at his side, holding on to his paws. His eyes weren't fully closed, but his eyelids twitched and his eyes rolled.

"Grub's here, Thorn," said Mud. "You're going to be all right." His paws were shaking as they cupped one of Thorn's.

"Let me see him," said Grub, gently moving Moth away from Thorn. "What happened?"

"Snakebite," said Moth. "I think it was a black mamba."

Grub didn't respond for a second. He carried on examining

Thorn's arm, which was scraped and swollen. "I need herbs," he said at last. "If I'd known before I left—but they grow near here, I'll be back very soon. Keep him as comfortable as you can."

He scurried away into the trees, and Prance let out a heavy breath. She realized Mud was staring at her again, still with that look of deep distrust, and she shifted uncomfortably. Was he angry that she'd taken so long? She'd fetched the Goodleaf as fast as she could.

Moth seemed to notice Mud's glare and muttered something to him, drawing his attention. Prance didn't hear what Mud said back, but whatever it was, it sent Moth skittering away from him.

Is there something going on with him? Prance wondered, but then she chided herself. Of course there was—his best friend and Great Father was sick, maybe dying.

"Didn't mean to frighten you back there," said a voice, and she looked around to see Gallant sitting nearby. He looked a little awkward.

"You didn't," Prance told him, which was almost true. "I understand."

"If news spreads that the Great Father is incapacitated," Gallant said, "creatures will panic. They'll assume he's dying. And if they're right, and he doesn't wake up . . ."

Prance cringed. She had known Thorn for only a few days, but she had already grown so fond of him she couldn't bear to think of him dying.

"But the Goodleaf will help him, right?" she asked.

Gallant huffed through his nose. "I have no idea. But I do know that if Thorn leaves Bravelands without a Great Parent, there'll be chaos. The last time that happened, it was a catastrophe. If we're heading into those times again, I think it's better that most creatures not know it until they absolutely need to."

Prance looked around at the forest. It was still quite exposed here, each tree separated from the next by two or three gazelle-lengths. Any passing animal would see the tiny, huddled form at the base of the tree. "We need to get him back to the clearing," she said.

"Even at the clearing, we'll need help." Mud looked up. "If you want to be useful, go back to the baboons. Tell Cashew what's happening—*only* Cashew—and get her to send some trusted Highleaves to guard him."

"I'll go now," Prance said.

Prance was used to walking long distances with the herd, and there had been plenty of days when they had run for their lives more than once, but she felt exhaustion creeping over her as she made her way back through the forest with a handful of baboon Highleaves at her heels. Cashew had chosen four of them to return with her to guard the Great Father: Crab, Cricket, Acanthus, and Egg. Each of them looked strong, and they hurried through the twilight forest in front of her, anxious to get to the Great Father's side.

They were almost there when weariness suddenly overtook

Prance. She slowed to a halt, just for a moment, tossing her head to stretch out her neck.

As she looked ahead to where the Highleaves were walking through the leaves, instead of seeing them advancing away from her into the trees as she'd expected, she could see them just as clear and close as before.

But they were still moving, and she was not—or rather, she could feel her hooves planted in the soft earth, but she could also *see*, as if in a waking dream, herself passing by the baboons and overtaking them. For a moment she felt dizzy and panicked, wondering if somehow the trees were moving past her, instead of the other way around.

Have I fallen asleep? she thought. *Am I dreaming? Perhaps all of this is a bad dream. . . . Perhaps I'll wake up and find Thorn is fine. . . .*

Then she emerged into the Great Parent's clearing—though she didn't, she was still standing motionless in the forest—and saw Mud, Grub, Moth, and Gallant there, with a still-unconscious Thorn. They had moved him while she was away. Grub was tending his wound, rubbing it with a chewed-up, bright green paste of leaves, and Gallant was standing guard over him. Mud and Moth were farther away, and as Prance approached, she saw that they bent over a pile of scattered stones.

Just like they were talking about on the way to the Gathering, she thought. *They must be trying to read Thorn's future in the stones. . . .*

She trotted forward and opened her mouth to greet them, to tell them she'd brought the Highleaves.

"I just don't believe it!" Moth burst out. "How can Prance be responsible?"

Prance twitched to a halt, her jaw dropping.

"I don't like it either," Mud said. "But I see no other way to interpret what's happening. My vision was right. Prance is dangerous. She will be the death of the Great Father."

Moth shook her head. Mud ran his hands over his face.

"I should have made sure she went back to her herd," he groaned. "I should never have let her stay. I knew, and I did nothing! And now Thorn . . ."

"I still don't see it," Moth muttered. "I see death, yes. I see a gazelle and the Great Father. But I can't ignore what I see in the real world either, and all of this can't be her fault, it just doesn't make sense."

"It will," Mud said darkly. "We must watch her. If she has passed her death curse on to Thorn somehow . . ."

Prance let out a shaky breath through her muzzle and started forward. She couldn't stand here and listen to this. She wasn't responsible, and she wasn't *cursed*—Thorn had said so himself!

But she didn't get very far before she stopped again. Mud looked up, and he should have been looking right at her . . . but his gaze skimmed over her as if she wasn't there. She looked over her shoulder and realized he was looking at Grub, tending to Thorn. He hadn't reacted to her presence at all.

"Mud?" she said, moving so that she was standing right between him and Thorn. Mud still didn't react. But Moth looked up from the stones, a frown on her face. She tilted her head, looking around the clearing.

"Is someone there?" she said.

Prance stared at her. She moved her head, trying to catch Moth's eye, but it was as though Moth could see *something* in the space Prance occupied but couldn't focus on it.

I'm not really here, Prance thought. *This is a dream, or . . . or something.*

She looked down for the first time, trying to see her own hooves. But instead of fur and bone, all she saw was shadow. . . .

Then the world swam and darkened, and when she blinked to clear her vision, she wasn't in the clearing, she was standing in the forest. Three of the four Highleaves had gone on ahead, but one—Egg, who had a large, bald forehead—was lingering, watching her. He tilted his head curiously.

"Are you all right, Prance?" he asked. Prance nodded and shook herself. Her legs felt stiff, but she managed to trot on and catch up with him.

"Just tired," she said. "I think I fell asleep on my feet for a second."

She put her head down as they pressed on, her horns feeling heavy.

Just a dream. I'm not cursed. I didn't do this.

But when she stepped out from the trees, she saw Grub tending to Thorn, that same bright green pulp in his hands. She saw Gallant standing guard exactly where he had been. Moth had moved to sit by herself on the other side of the clearing, but Mud was still in the same spot, and when he looked up and saw Prance, she noticed he quickly scooped up his pile of stones and set them aside.

It was all the same. What she'd seen and heard while she was frozen in the forest—all of it was real.

But *how*?

CHAPTER TWELVE

Chase paused, catching her breath and scenting the air. She had followed the scent of Seek, the warm cub smell overlaid with something foul and rotten—the scent of the snakebite. It wasn't hard to trace him, but no matter how quickly she scrambled up the mountainside, she couldn't seem to catch him. She felt a pang of guilt for leaving Shadow alone, again. Every few pawsteps she felt sure she must be about to find Seek, and even if that wasn't true, she couldn't turn back now.

How could Seek have gotten so far, so fast? Wasn't he hurt? Or had the madness overwhelmed his senses?

She didn't want to believe what the hyena had said, but as hard as she tried, she couldn't find another explanation for Seek's awful mood, his aggressive behavior, and now this.

She put on another burst of speed, but even leaping from rock to rock and using all her weight to shoulder through the underbrush, there was no sign that she was catching up to him.

All of a sudden, the trail vanished from in front of her nose. She skidded to a halt, panic raising the hairs along her back. But then she realized it hadn't vanished at all—Seek had just taken a sharp turn to the east.

He runs like he knows exactly where he's going, she thought. *Where could he* . . .

No.

She stared, frozen to the spot, her ears pinned back in horror. He wouldn't, would he? Why would he go *there*?

Perhaps the madness was driving him back to the place where it had begun. Perhaps he was just heading toward the strongest leopard he knew. But if Chase didn't get to him before he made it to Range's cave, he wouldn't make it out alive.

Chase broke into a sprint, pushing herself to run faster and faster. She abandoned Seek's trail, certain now that she knew where he was going, and leaped up into the trees to run along the branches, cutting off corners wherever she could. She scanned the ground below as she sprang from one tree to the next, but there was still no sign of Seek.

At last she reached the edge of the rushing river, where the huge gray stones jutted out into the fast-moving water, and the waterfall ahead of her splashed and churned. She shuddered as she remembered the impact of that water, when she had thrown herself and Seek out into the river, to escape from Range and his snakes. She remembered the older leopard's strangely calm demeanor, the odd things he'd said as the snakes advanced to spread their madness to Seek. . . .

Oh. Chase felt a chill in her paws as she hurried up the stone path toward the waterfall. *Range must have it too. The snakes must have bitten him. That's why he tolerated them in his cave. . . . That's why he brought us to them. . . .*

Is that why Seek's leading me here now? Is this a trap?

But she couldn't think like that. She had to be ready for whatever she found in Range's den behind the waterfall. If she had to fight off Range and his snakes all by herself and drag Seek out of there by force, she would do it.

The cliffside was slick and cold with spray from the waterfall, and Chase forced herself to slow down as she picked her way along it. If she fell, or charged into the cave unprepared, there was no telling what might happen to Seek. At the point where the path met the curtain of roaring water, she actually stopped and shook herself, tensing her muscles, picking her moment. Then she sprang into the darkness, teeth bared and snarling.

She skidded to a stop on the dark stone, her paws spread to balance herself, ready to snap and tear at any snake foolish enough to come near her.

But there was no hissing, no movement. The only sound was the dying echo of her own snarl, and the crashing of the waterfall outside. Her eyes adjusted quickly to the darkness, and she scanned every corner of the cave that she could see, looking for the telltale creeping of a snake's body. She looked up at the high rock where Range had sat to watch the attack before, and it was deserted.

No Range, no snakes, and no Seek. The cub's scent was here, though. He *had* come this way. Gingerly, she raised herself from her battle-ready crouch and sniffed at the ground, half-afraid she would find that Seek's trail ended in a pool of blood. But it just carried on, into the deeper recesses of the cave.

Chase shuddered. But she couldn't stop now. Carefully watching where she put her paws, she stalked into the darkness, passing under a low arch of rocks. On the other side, a pitch-black tunnel wound through the rock, sloping upward. Even with her leopard's vision, Chase's eyes failed her, and she walked for a few hesitant pawsteps in pitch blackness, with only Seek's familiar-yet-unfamiliar scent to guide her.

Then, at last, she found she could dimly see the shapes of the rocks in front of her. The tunnel twisted once again, and she found herself at the bottom of a slope that led up to a crevice in the rock, large enough for a leopard to slip through. All she could see on the other side was a pale light, as if it opened out into the sky.

She hurried up the slope and pushed through the gap.

On the other side, she found herself standing on a rocky shelf, beside a river—looking back, she realized the tunnel had led her up to the top of the waterfall. Beyond the rising spray, she could see out over the forest, all the way to the plains. And on the other side of her, the river snaked up into the higher mountains, where the clouds lay thick between the dripping trees.

Seek's scent was here, but so was Range's. There was no

blood spilled. Just a twining trail of both scents that led up into the forest.

Where has Range taken him? Chase wondered miserably. *What kind of sickness can make someone behave like this?*

She set off to follow the trail, her paws feeling heavier than before, though she still tried to hurry. Would she ever find Seek again? What would she do when she did?

She had gone only a little way into the trees when she smelled something else that raised her hackles.

Gorillas! She looked around. *That's right. . . . If I'd gone around another way, I'd have come to the edge of their territory where I met that young gorilla.*

Some of the energy and urgency returned to her, and she picked up the pace. If the gorillas caught a leopard trespassing on their territory, they wouldn't pause to ask where she was going. If Range and Seek refused to leave . . .

Chase tried not to think about the sight of her mother, Prowl, lying where she had died, gorillas throwing rocks and punching at her corpse in their fury that she had taken one of their own with her. Chase had never understood why Prowl had gone into the gorilla territory in the first place. And now Seek and Chase were both running right into the same danger.

She took to the trees again as she drew closer to the center of the gorillas' territory, knowing that she could just as easily meet one of the lumbering creatures up in the branches, but at least then they wouldn't be able to drop down on her unexpectedly. As she pressed up the slope, leaping from one tree to the next, the scents of gorillas grew thicker and more oppressive, until she knew she was right in the heart of their territory. But there was something odd here.

There were no gorillas.

She knew, from creeping here once or twice and from Prowl's teachings, that gorillas would normally stay near their nests for most of the day. They ate plants, nuts, and fruit that grew in abundance nearby, so there should have been at least a few of them around. Chase could see the flattened leaves where the gorillas slept on the forest floor, and a few nests in the trees where they had dragged up soft moss and ferns and packed them into the crooks of the branches. She stepped up to one and sniffed at it gingerly. It wasn't abandoned—its owner had been here recently, had probably slept here last night. . . .

But where are they now?

Chase shuddered. She didn't like this emptiness.

Just then, she heard a howling and tensed, digging her claws into the tree branch. It sounded like a gorilla's cry, but there was something strange about it. Another voice joined it, and then another, until the forest shook with the hollering of gorillas.

Seek!

She hurried toward the sound, as fast as she could go without drawing attention to herself, padding on silent paws, keeping her belly low to the tree branches.

Suddenly, she came to the edge of this part of the forest and cringed back into the shadows of the tree as she looked down at a great ridge of black stone. Chase lay on the branch, trying to take it all in. She had never seen anything quite like this. Jagged rock spurs stuck up from the ground. One of them had a deep hole running through it into darkness, and a thin stream of something leaked up into the air from beneath. It must be mist, or steam.

The gorilla troop was here. They had gathered in a great circle, hooting and pounding their chests.

She recognized a few of them, from that awful day when Prowl had died.

But she couldn't see Seek anywhere. A tiny spark of hope lit up in her chest. Surely there would be chaos if he and Range were here? Surely she would see their bodies if they'd already been killed?

Then the thumping of the gorilla's chests seemed to grow more regular, and the howls changed into something else, something that chilled Chase's blood.

Hissing.

One by one, each of the gorillas started hissing like—well, like a snake. They swayed, their heads rolling from side to side, almost as if their bodies weren't under their control. The hissing rose like the steam from the ground and surrounded Chase. Her hackles raised and her paws prickled. She instinctively backed away, hunching her shoulders and resisting the urge to open her jaws and hiss back at them. Her whole body was telling her to run, but she couldn't listen. She had to find Seek, and now she was sure that meant learning what was going on here.

Burbark Silverback emerged from the circle, climbing up onto one of the jutting black rocks. He held up his hands, and the gorillas stopped thumping their chests all at once.

"Friends," the Silverback said. "It is a good day. A joyful day. This day, we welcome another to our number."

A few of the gorillas let out another hiss, apparently in agreement.

"We have lost two of our kind to the bloody plains, but we have mourned their betrayal, and those who could not stop them have atoned for their failure. We will speak of them no more. Instead, we will celebrate."

He bent down to the edge of the rock, picked something up in one hand, and raised it up for the others to see.

It was Seek.

Chase sprang to her paws and ran to the edge of the branch. These things were about to kill Seek, as part of some horrible snake ritual! She had to stop them, she had to—

But Seek was speaking.

"I have heard Her call," he said, his voice thin and strange. He lay still in the gorilla's gentle grip, no trace of the fury that had turned him against her and Shadow. "I have seen the truth. I pledge my life to serve Grandmother!"

"Welcome to the family, son," Burbark said and raised his other hand. A snake had wrapped itself around his arm, and it lashed out, quick as lightning, and bit Seek on the paw.

"No!" Chase howled. As one, with the speed of snakes, the gorillas' heads turned to stare at her. She hissed with fury and panic, torn between running away and leaping down to claw at them until either she could steal Seek back from this awful "family" or they killed her, just like they killed Prowl. . . .

Then there was movement among them, and Range stepped from the group. The gorillas parted to let him through.

The Silverback drew Seek to his chest, cradling him as if he was his own cub. "Get her," he said.

Range advanced, and Chase made up her mind. She turned and ran.

What are you doing? some part of her mind was yelling at her in disbelief, telling her to turn back, that she couldn't leave Seek, that she would rather die. But Chase shut out the voice. She leaped and clawed her way through the trees, throwing aside her caution.

Beneath her, she heard the thumping of Range's big paws in the leaves, and then a scraping sound, and then the rustling of branches. He was in the trees, right behind her. She didn't look. She kept her gaze fixed on the next branch, and the next, until she heard the sound of rushing water and ran down a tree trunk and out into the open, onto the rocks by the waterfall. She spun around and looked back, searching the trees for the leaping shape of a leopard. She didn't see him. She backed toward the entrance to the cave tunnel, hoping that if she could just make it inside, if she had to, she could escape the same way she had before—out through Range's cave and the leap into the water. . . .

Then she sensed something moving in the undergrowth. By the time she reacted, it was too late. Range was in mid-leap.

His paws struck Chase's shoulder and rolled her onto her

back on the damp stone. Chase spat and clawed at him, but he was stronger and heavier and he had her pinned, one paw on her ribs, another on her throat. She could smell the *wrongness* on him now, the same foul wounded smell that Seek had had. It was older and fainter, but unmistakable.

"Why?" she yowled. "Why are you doing this?" She tried to snap at his foreleg, desperate to get away before he sank his teeth into her throat. But he didn't.

"I won't kill you," Range said. "It would be a waste."

"Then let me go!" Chase snapped.

"Not until you say you'll stay," Range said. "Stop struggling and listen to me."

Against all her instincts, Chase forced herself to go still. She thought of the prey creatures who would play dead to make predators think they were already rot-meat.

"Tell me, then!" she panted. "What is happening? What has happened to Seek?"

"Nothing bad," said Range. "He had to be bitten, to join the gorillas as I have, in the service of a higher power! It doesn't hurt after the first time, and afterward . . . the power it gives you, Chase. The *insight*. After you've submitted to Her bite, you will understand."

Chase stared into Range's eyes and found nothing there but deep, cold sincerity. He believed every word he was saying.

"In the service of She of a Thousand Skins, you will be rewarded when the Age of Sandtongue comes," Range went on. "If you don't come now, willingly, I won't be able to protect you when it's time for Her final reckoning. Now is the time, Chase. Choose the right side and survive. If you won't do it for me, do it for Seek. He's one of her chosen now. His fate is tied to Grandmother, as is mine."

"I . . . I can't think like this," Chase panted. "Please, let me up."

Range stepped off her, and she waited as long as she could bear to before scrambling to her paws and backing away. Range didn't follow her.

"I won't hurt you," he said, and his expression turned to sadness. "There is nothing you can do to stop the Age of Sandtongue coming. I will let you go, but if you do, remember there will always be a place for you among the chosen."

"I'll take my chances out here," she snarled. "But if any harm comes to my cub . . ."

"Seek is with his family now," said Range. Chase felt as if he had dug his claws into her stomach.

"*I* am his family!" she yowled.

"No harm will befall him," Range said, ignoring her outburst. "I give you my word. And I hope to see you again very soon."

He turned his back on her, and she watched, pressed against the rocks with her fur crawling, as he walked away.

CHAPTER THIRTEEN

The kopje was a strange place to be, after the endless flatness of the plain they'd just crossed. Bramble and Moonflower had decided it would be quicker to go up and over rather than around it, so suddenly and briefly they were back on familiar ground, clambering over rocks and around trees.

The grass had been growing thicker and greener as they'd approached the kopje, which made Bramble feel a little more at home, and a lot more cautious. It was a relief to be back where there was water, but the long grass could easily hide some new terrifying plains creature that would be much less friendly than the elephants.

They reached the low summit of the kopje, and Bramble paused to look out at what was on the other side. Sure enough, there was a forest! It was odd to see a forest that was so flat, but it looked enormous, deep and dark and homely, and Bramble's heart swelled to know that the Great Father was somewhere inside.

There was just one problem with the elephants' directions.

"So . . . she didn't think to mention the *river*?" Moonflower said.

"I guess for giants like them, it's more like a stream," Bramble said. But it was definitely a river, winding silver cutting in front of the forest. It was wide enough that the gorillas would probably have to swim across, and it was definitely in their way.

"We'd better get going," Moonflower said. "It looks like it's a bit narrower over there, let's head in that direction."

Bramble agreed wholeheartedly. He didn't want a long swim. He wondered if Moonflower was thinking the same as he was—there were worse things that could happen to them in the water than being washed away. He kept seeing the blind lizard in his mind's eye, lurching up over the side of the gully.

They made their way down to the edge of the water, Bramble moving more and more gingerly as they came to the river. The banks weren't as steep as they had been in the gully, and he couldn't see any hollows where lizards could be lurking—but then, he hadn't seen them until it was too late last time, either.

"Hey, look," said Moonflower, pointing a little upstream. "There's a big rock in the river over there."

Bramble looked and saw the rounded, mottled stone she was pointing at.

"If we cross there, we can stop halfway if we need to. Let's do it," he agreed.

The two gorillas hurried upstream until they were level with the rock, and Bramble took a deep breath and waded into the water. He had crossed mountain streams before. He and Cassava had even dared each other to wade into the river that ran into the waterfall, much to Apple's horror when she found out. This river wasn't even moving very fast. It wasn't so bad.

Then the water reached his waist, and then his shoulders, and then his toes lost their grip on the mud beneath him and he was bobbing, untethered in the water.

It's bad!

He just had to get to the rock. It was only a few leopard-lengths away. He looked back as Moonflower sank into the water next to him, and then started trying to push and kick through the water.

It was much harder than it looked. He tried not to panic, but it was a huge relief when he reached out one hand to grab on to the rock.

There was something strange about it, though. It wasn't the smooth stone texture he was expecting. His hand slapped down on something yielding, almost soft. He managed to pull himself up and reached down to help Moonflower up after him.

"What is that smell?" Moonflower gasped, reaching for his hand. "What is this thing?" She leant down to sniff at the surface of the little island.

"This thing is not a *thing*!" growled a deep, bubbly voice from right below Bramble's feet. He jumped and spun around, slipping on the slick and squishy surface, to see a head rising from the water, small round ears flicking with anger and a bulbous nose snorting water. A small black eye, ringed with long, wet lashes, turned to squint at the two gorillas, and then the rock—the creature's back—shifted under Bramble's feet and he found himself tossed back into the water, right on top of Moonflower. He was plunged under the surface and saw what had been hidden from above—a huge body, four enormous feet, and a pair of jaws that opened to show off a row of gigantic chomping teeth.

He struggled back to the surface of the water, grabbed Moonflower, and started desperately thrashing his way back to the bank. He thought they weren't going to make it, but the creature was slow to turn, and it pushed the water in front of it so that Bramble actually found himself shoved along by the ripples. He clawed at the water until his toes found purchase in the mud. Moonflower was right alongside him, and together they charged out of the water, sopping wet and muddy. He looked back and let out a terrified yelp as he realized the enormous creature wasn't stopping at the edge of the river either—it took a few pounding steps up onto the muddy bank and roared at them.

"Stay out of my river!" it yelled.

Bramble nodded hard. "I'm sorry!" he yelped. He just hoped it was enough—he was certain this animal could run them down and crush them in a moment if it wanted to.

The creature snorted again and sank slowly backward into the water.

"Better hope I never see you here again," it muttered, before half vanishing back underneath the surface.

Moonflower sucked in a breath. "What was *that*?" she hissed.

"Hippopotamus," said a voice.

Bramble startled, slipped in the mud, and almost fell over in his hurry to turn around. Standing behind them was an elderly-looking monkey, much skinnier and a bit shorter than them. He was balding and hunched, patches of his leathery skin showing under his fur, and there was a little bird sitting on his shoulder. As they watched, he sat down on the ground and opened his mouth, and the bird hopped closer and began to pick at his teeth.

Moonflower thumped the ground with her knuckles, seemingly annoyed at being startled by such an odd monkey. "Hippo-*what*-amus?" she demanded.

The monkey gestured to the bird and shrugged, as if he couldn't possibly interrupt its important job.

Bramble just stared at him, lost for words.

After an awkward pause, the bird hopped out and started picking at something on the ground instead.

"Thank you," said the monkey, apparently to the bird, and licked his teeth. "I said, *hippopotamus*. That's the big angry thing you two mistook for a rock. Grumpy at the best of times. Not the best choice on your part."

"And who and what are you?" Moonflower demanded.

"I'm a baboon, or so they tell me," said the stranger.

Bramble and Moonflower looked at each other. A baboon . . . an elderly baboon, who seemed friendly with birds and knew about hippopotamuses . . .

"Are you . . . you're not . . . the Great Father, are you?" Bramble asked.

"Ha!" The baboon slapped the ground and cackled. "I'm *a* father, but not a great one, I'm afraid. Moth's the one you want."

"The Great Father's name is Moth?"

"No, no, Moth's my daughter," said the baboon.

Bramble sighed. He had a sinking feeling that they had picked entirely the wrong baboon to talk to.

"She *lives* with Great Father Thorn," the baboon went on.

"Oh!" Bramble was pleased to hear it, but no less confused.

"Now, I've introduced Moth and Thorn, and they're not even here. Let's do us too. My name is Spider." The baboon tapped his chest. "And you two gorillas are a long way from your troop."

"You know about gorillas?" Bramble asked.

"And where's *your* troop?" Moonflower said. Bramble could tell she was still a bit cross, and he couldn't blame her—this baboon was being very strange.

"I have no troop. I like to travel. Become other things. I've been to the mountain," Spider said. "I saw the gorillas there, and you two are gorillas, no mistaking your great big heads. I'm a crocodile at the moment—or, I was," he said, frowning.

Bramble glanced at Moonflower, wondering if he'd misheard. Did this baboon just claim to *be* a crocodile?

"Oh, I know what you're thinking. Spider's crazy. But I am not. The crocodiles accepted me and didn't eat me, just like the plovers. I had a son for a while, Chew—raised him from an egg. But the crocodiles have gone now."

"Gone?" Bramble asked before he could stop himself. He could feel himself being pulled in, and he could tell Moonflower would rather he hadn't asked.

"Vanished," said Spider. Bramble waited, but this time it seemed one word was all Spider needed.

Considering he thought of himself as a crocodile, he doesn't seem particularly worried by this, he thought. Then he shook himself. *Considering he thinks he's a crocodile, maybe we shouldn't be listening to him.*

"Well, I'm Moonflower, and this is Bramble, and we need to see the Great Father," Moonflower said. "Which means we need to get across this river, so if you'll excuse us, we need to find somewhere out of sight of that grumpy creature to try to swim across."

"Oh, there are other ways to get to the other side of the river," said Spider.

Moonflower gave Bramble a deeply skeptical look. "Yes?"

"Well, you could fly," said Spider. "If you could find an eagle willing to carry you. Maybe four or five for you two."

"Uh-huh," said Moonflower. "I think we'll be better off figuring this out by ourselves, thanks."

"You could wait here until the hot season, and then walk across when the water goes down," Spider went on, as if he hadn't heard her. "*Or . . .* well, you don't have to *cross* a river to get to the other side. Come with me."

He picked up a stick from the ground beside him and hobbled away.

"We should just leave him to it," Moonflower muttered, watching him go.

Bramble sighed. "You might be right, but . . . what if he actually knows another way across? We need to find one. Let's just wait and see if he's doing something that's . . ."

He trailed off as he watched Spider walk over to a spot near a big boulder and thump the ground with his stick, then with his hands. Then he started jumping up and down on the spot, stomping the earth with his feet.

"All right, perhaps we should go," Bramble said.

"Found it!" Spider called out. He jammed the stick into the ground and started to dig at a mound of earth, until he'd loosened it enough to start digging with his paws. He looked up at the gorillas. "You could help, you know."

Moonflower rolled her eyes, but she went up to Spider and started digging beside him. Bramble went after them and dug his hands in too.

At this point, why not? he thought.

"I'm not digging all the way under this river," Moonflower told Spider as she threw earth out behind her.

"No, not at all," Spider said cheerfully. "In fact, we're almost . . . ah!"

All of a sudden, the layer of earth fell away, and Bramble felt a cool empty space under his hands.

He peered down at the hole. The inside was dark, but he could make out that it widened and continued down into a tunnel just about big enough for them to crawl through.

"This goes under the river?" he asked in amazement.

"It goes to lots of places," said Spider smugly. But then, perhaps in response to the glare Moonflower gave him, he pointed across the river. "One of those places is under that clump of bushes over there. Come on! I'll show you."

And with barely a look back, the old baboon bent over and slid headfirst into the hole.

Bramble steeled himself and followed. He had to push aside some more earth to fit his shoulders into the hole, but he did fit, just. And once he was inside, the ground under his hands was hardened, like stone, and he could make out that the path ahead was a tunnel that led down into the earth. He found it was possible to knuckle forward if he kept his head down.

Behind him, he heard the sound of earth moving, and then Moonflower's soft grunt as she dropped down into the tunnel.

"It's not too far," Spider said. "Just make sure you stay close behind me."

"We're here," Bramble said.

It was a relief to find that the tunnel really did seem to go somewhere, deep into the earth. That was about all the positivity Bramble could find, after a few minutes of crawling in the dark. It was chilly and damp, and his senses were dulled, with nothing to see or smell in any direction except mud. He kept bumping his shoulders and head on the walls, and before long he started to feel desperately homesick for the mountain, with its open sky and fresh scents.

He tried to guess how far they'd gone, but it was almost impossible. Were they underneath the river right now? What if the tunnel gave way and the water rushed in?

"You said these tunnels go to lots of places," he said, desperate to distract himself from that train of thought. "How far do they go?"

"All over Bravelands," said Spider. "All the way to the mountain, I think. I've tried to get that far, but I always get lost."

Lost? That's not something I wanted to hear right now.

"What made them?" said Moonflower, her voice slightly muffled behind him.

"Water, I think," Spider said. "Some are dry, some are full up with lovely sloshing water. Some are full of moles and meerkats," he added. "And dogs and lizards. Comfy underground burrows, these are."

Bramble did not feel comfy. Not just because they had to squeeze through a narrow gap as the tunnel suddenly split into two and Spider led them down and to the right, but because of Spider's words.

An underground burrow for lizards that goes where the water is, all the way to the mountain, he thought. *Back in that gully, the lizard seemed to come up out of the ground. But it couldn't be connected . . . could it?*

It couldn't possibly be much farther, could it? They must be right underneath the river by now, if not out the other side. The tunnel wound this way and that, and Bramble suppressed a frustrated groan every time it turned, knowing that it must be adding time to the journey. Even though the stone around him was damp, he soon found himself dry-mouthed with nerves.

"Hmm," said Spider, coming to a halt suddenly, so that Bramble almost knuckled into his hairless red behind.

"What? What is it?" Moonflower called.

Spider was muttering to himself. "Don't think . . . shouldn't be a turn here . . . maybe it was the left fork . . ."

Is he lost?!

Panic threatened to overwhelm Bramble. If he'd been able to see, his vision would have been swimming. He felt like the tunnel was spinning underneath him. He hunkered down and tried to control his breathing.

"No problems," Spider said at last. "Possible we might come out somewhere else. That's fine."

And with that, he set off again. Bramble tried to follow, but his limbs didn't seem to respond to his instructions.

"It's okay, Bramble. He's not wrong," Moonflower said in a surprisingly soothing voice. "We can't go backward, so we'll just keep going until we find another way out."

"Yeah, you're right," Bramble said, hoping that if he said it out loud he would believe it more. "Next time I might take my chances with the hippopotamus, though."

Suddenly, up ahead, Bramble saw something. Light was filtering in from somewhere, and his heart swelled, thinking that they might finally be about to get out of this horrible place. The tunnel grew slightly bigger, and Bramble looked up and saw a few small holes in the ceiling. There were ants underfoot, and he thought they must be right below an abandoned anthill.

Past the river, then, unless they'd circled around on

themselves. He still couldn't see the end of the tunnel, though. Just the faint shape of Spider in front of him, and over Spider's shoulder, the rest of the tunnel . . . and something else. Bramble squinted. It was a strange shape, knobbly and elongated.

Then it moved, and Bramble shuffled back, bumping into Moonflower, as he saw the shape open up to show faint white teeth and a gleaming yellow eye. For a moment he thought it really was the lizard from the gully, but it was a different shape, longer and darker.

"Gnash," Spider said. "There you are! What are you doing down here? Is Chew with you?"

The crocodile advanced. Bramble held his breath, waiting for some kind of response . . . but there was none.

"Gnash?" Spider said. His normal cheerful tone had turned doubtful, and Bramble's skin crawled. "Wait . . ."

But the crocodile kept coming, eyes wide and staring.

CHAPTER FOURTEEN

Prance sat at the edge of the Great Father's clearing, watching the sheltered alcove where Thorn was lying out of sight, tended by the Goodleaf and guarded by Highleaves. Mud was in there too. He hadn't let Prance see Thorn.

Prance is dangerous. She will be the death of the Great Father.

Mud's words echoed in her mind as she watched Moth scamper in and out, bringing handfuls of various berries and leaves. She hadn't been allowed to help with that, either. Mud probably thought she would poison the Great Father if she was involved.

She still had no idea how or why she had seen him say it, but she had to face the fact that he *might* be right. She *could* have brought some curse upon the Great Father.

But I'm not the only thing that's strange in Bravelands.

Even if she was carrying a curse or a bad omen, that didn't

explain the snakes. They had swarmed on Great Father, different species all moving together, all with the same purpose, and as soon as one of them had managed to bite Thorn, the rest had melted away into the grass. Prance had never seen anything like it before.

And there was her nightmare, of her herd turning into snake-creatures. There was the strange behavior of the crocodiles, and there was Broadsight, the giraffe leader, who'd been bitten by something and turned erratic. How many more of the strange tales that the creatures of Bravelands were bringing to the Great Father could be traced back to some kind of sandtongue creature?

With Thorn in such desperate need of help—maybe even dying—nobody was looking for the source of the problem.

But I can.

She made up her mind not to tell Mud what she was thinking, and after a short time agonizing, she decided against telling Moth either. She was sure Moth would understand, but Grub would need her help for a while yet. And Prance didn't think she should tell Gallant either. If she turned up where she was going with a lion in tow . . . it seemed more likely to put both of them in danger than a gazelle by herself.

No, Prance would go alone. She'd been alone before.

She waited until Gallant got up from his position on the other side of the clearing and headed off alone, telling Prance to stay in the clearing while he tended to his pride. She gave him a little while to get out of the forest, then she got up and slipped away. It was easy enough. She glanced back as she left the clearing, but none of the baboons were watching her.

Am I doing the right thing? she thought as she left the shadow of the trees and walked out onto the grassy plain. *What if Mud's correct, and whatever I do, I'm doomed to hurt Thorn?*

Well, if that's true, there's nothing I can do to avoid it, she countered. *I won't sit back there and let him die because I'm afraid of making it worse.*

It didn't take her too long to find what she was looking for, even in the vastness of the plains. She asked a few passing animals to point her in the right direction—even a serval cat, feeling very brave at approaching a predator, though the predator in question came up only to her knees. But she had just left the cat, who assured her she was getting close to her destination, when she suddenly felt a prickling on the back of her neck and spun around.

Nothing moved in the grass, but Prance stood still for a moment, ears swiveling, ready to bolt if she saw anything slithering or creeping up on her. Eventually she pulled herself away, but the feeling of being watched still bothered her, until finally she rounded a large rock and saw the giraffe herd.

They were gathered around a copse of large trees, as she'd expected, but as she approached them, she saw that there was something wrong here. The trees were almost completely stripped of their leaves. Why would the giraffes still be here, rather than moving on to find more food? They were pacing around with their heads bowed, muttering to one another, or leaning listlessly against the tree trunks. And there was something dark sprawled in the grass a little way away, which

Prance realized was a dead hyena, swarming with flies.

Avoiding the corpse, she approached the herd. Skywatch looked up and saw her, and she saw a heavy expression lift from his face.

"Friends!" he said, trotting over to another giraffe and nudging them with his big, flat head. "Look! The Great Father has sent us an emissary!"

Prance flushed. *It wouldn't help them to know the truth*, she thought. She tried to walk like an emissary of the Great Spirit, as Skywatch loped up to meet her with the rest of the herd on his heels.

"My name is Prance. The Great Father sends his best wishes for your herd," she said. "How does your leader fare, Skywatch?" She craned her neck to look up at the faces of the tall creatures who surrounded her. Was one of them Broad-sight? None of them stood out as a leader, and she couldn't see any snakebites on their legs either.

"He . . ." Skywatch heaved a great sigh. "He's not telling us we need to go to the mountain anymore. It's worse than that now."

"He has declared *war* on the hyenas," said a female giraffe, her expression grim.

"What? Why?" Prance frowned. That made no sense—no plant-eater herd animal would start a fight with a predator, not without a very good reason, and especially not against creatures who weren't usually much of a threat.

The giraffes looked at one another awkwardly. Prance got

the impression that it wasn't that they couldn't explain it, but that none of them wanted to. At last, Skywatch seemed to accept that it was going to be his job.

"He says we have a mission," Skywatch said. "He says it's because they're rot-meat-eaters, and that makes them our enemies. None of us understand it!"

"If they eat rot-meat, that makes them less of a danger to us than the lions, right?" said another giraffe.

"He's determined to pursue this war of his, and meanwhile the rest of us are getting hungry," said Skywatch. "It doesn't make any sense, but he won't move the herd now, even though we've begged him. We . . . we're thinking about moving on without him. Broadsight's leadership might have come to an end, just like Great Father said."

All the giraffes bowed their heads in sadness.

"But there must be something the Great Spirit can do to help my father," piped up a small voice, from much closer to Prance's own head height. She peered between the spindly legs of the giraffes and saw a much smaller one—taller than she was, but obviously still a foal—looking at her with large, innocent eyes.

She felt a pang of guilt. She couldn't do anything on behalf of the Great Spirit, except gather information. She certainly couldn't save this poor foal's father all by herself. But perhaps if she saw Broadsight herself, she would think of a way.

"Where is your father now?" she asked the young giraffe. He looked up at Skywatch, who nodded.

"Why don't you take her to see him, Shortsight?" he said.

"All right. Follow me," said Shortsight, and the other giraffes parted to let them through. Prance glanced back and saw, with a little apprehension, that they were all staying behind, blinking after her with their long black lashes.

She walked after Shortsight, trying not to look nervous as he led her past the trees to the other side of the copse, where a lone giraffe came into view. His spots were the same reddish-brown shade as Shortsight's. He was standing perfectly still and staring, apparently at nothing. Prance squinted at the horizon, but she could make out very little between here and the blue shadow of the distant mountain.

That's right, Skywatch said he wanted to go there, she remembered. *But why?*

She immediately spotted the bite mark on Broadsight's leg. It looked like it was barely healing at all. The leg was swollen and red all around it, and the wound was wet, as if pus or venom was constantly leaking from it. Prance tried to suppress her shudder and took a deep breath.

"Good day, Broadsight," she said. "The Great Father sends his blessings to your herd. He sent me to ask if you feel better, after you were bitten by that snake."

Skywatch hadn't said it was a snake, so this was a gamble. But Broadsight didn't confirm or deny her speculation.

He blinked but didn't turn his head away from the mountain. "The Great Father isn't long for this world," he said.

Prance froze. *How does he know? Has the news gotten out already?*

No, it couldn't have—the other giraffes didn't seem to have any idea anything was wrong, and who else would have told him?

"The Great Father is in good health," she said, trying not to sound frightened, at least in front of Shortsight.

Broadsight scoffed but didn't reply.

"Shortsight, why don't you go back to the others?" Prance said. Shortsight backed away, nodding sadly. It hurt Prance's heart to see the way he looked at his father, hope dwindling with every moment. She waited until he turned, and then carefully walked around Broadsight until she could look him head-on, even if he wouldn't look down at her in return. "Broadsight, the code of Bravelands says only kill to survive— you remember that, don't you?"

The giraffe leader still didn't respond.

"You have every right to defend yourself, but the hyenas are no threat to your herd," she said.

"Survival can mean many things," said Broadsight.

Prance sighed. "Will you at least come back with me to the Great Father's clearing?" she asked. "Grub Goodleaf is there. He'll be able to help you with the snakebite." *And he'll be able to compare it to Thorn's*, she thought.

"Don't need help from a baboon," said Broadsight.

"I think you do," Prance insisted. "I think your wound is preventing you from seeing clearly."

Broadsight's head turned to look directly at Prance, so abruptly that she startled and danced a few hoofbeats backward. The movement reminded her, eerily, of a snake. He blinked, and she saw that his eyes were misty and clouded.

"I see more clearly than ever," he said. "I can see the future."

Prance shuddered and backed away even more.

"You should come to the clearing," she said. "Great Father wants to help you." And without waiting to hear what ominous comment he would make next, she turned and ran back around the trees to where she had left the other giraffes.

However, when she got to the spot, she looked around in confusion. The giraffes were all gone—all but Shortsight, who was standing, alone and forlorn-looking, by the trunk of the tree.

"What happened?" Prance asked. "They didn't just leave without you, did they?"

"No," said Shortsight in a small voice. "They waited. But I told them to go. I can't leave my father all alone."

Prance sighed, touched by his loyalty, but so sad for him that it was hard to speak. "I'm sorry, Shortsight. Your father needs more help than either of us can give him. You should go with the others. Come on," she said, looking out at the horizon. "We'll be able to catch them up. Which way did they—"

She broke off. She had seen something moving on the plain—but it wasn't the tall, lumbering giraffes. Pale brown shapes were slinking through the long grass toward them, short fur standing up along their rangy backs.

Hyenas!

Prance stepped close to Shortsight, trying not to panic. A full herd of giraffes might not find them much trouble, but a single gazelle and a giraffe foal were easy pickings for a hyena pack. She was about to tell Shortsight to run, but the shout died in her throat as she looked left and right and realized it was already much too late. There were at least six hyenas, ranged around them in a wide circle, and maybe more she couldn't make out still hidden in the grass.

They were surrounded.

"Poor little big thing," one of the hyenas chuckled. "Herd gone and left you all alone?"

"Prance?" Shortsight quavered.

"Get away from him," Prance said. She lowered her horns and tried to pretend to be brave. "The first one who jumps is going to face my horns, and I promise you, they're sharp!"

The hyenas cackled. One of them feinted forward, snapping its jaws in the air, and Prance let out a very un-brave squeak.

"Can't impale us all," said one of them.

Prance tried to get her brave face back, but she could hardly hear the hyenas' taunts over the sound of her blood pounding in her head. She was so foolish, and it was going to get her killed. If only she'd brought Gallant with her. If only she hadn't told the other giraffes to leave. If only she hadn't spent so long trying to talk to Broadsight . . .

She tried to keep her horns pointed at the closest hyenas, but they dodged and weaved and she couldn't keep track of them. Then she heard Shortsight hiss in pain and fear. She looked back to find a hyena that had crept up behind them, biting down on one of the foal's legs. She yelled and reared up, flailing at the hyena with her hooves. It let go and scampered away, giggling.

"Get away!" Shortsight yelled and made a brave attempt to stamp on the tail of a hyena who streaked past.

Prance felt the ground shake beneath her and saw several of the hyenas cringe back in fear. She looked around just in time to see Broadsight bearing down on them, froth flying from his mouth. He ran straight for the hyena that had Short-sight's blood on its mouth, and without hesitation or mercy, he brought his hooves down on the hyena's back. There was an awful *crunch*, and the creature crumpled into a still heap in the grass.

The other hyenas screeched and ran in circles, as if they wanted to run away, but couldn't bring themselves to leave.

"I will kill every last one of you, rot-eaters," Broadsight hissed.

"Hey!" one of the hyenas howled. She threw back her head and let out a high-pitched scream that seemed to bolster the others and calm their panic. "Look, look at its leg! This is the mad grass-eater! The one who's been killing our brothers and sisters!"

Prance's heart had already been in her hooves when she'd thought that she might be about to die, but somehow it still managed to sink as she realized what was about to happen. She hurriedly backed up against Shortsight's spindly legs and gently nudged him backward.

"We have to go," she whispered.

"But Father . . . ," Shortsight said.

Broadsight was still stamping his hooves into the ground around where the dead hyena lay, while the other hyenas gathered themselves around the one who'd howled out to them.

"It's time for our revenge!" she screamed.

"Revenge!" the other hyenas echoed. There was still laughter in their voices, but it was higher and more desperate now. "Murderer! Get him!"

They began to advance on Broadsight, spreading out carefully, circling and snapping at his legs.

"I will do my mistress's bidding until the end," Broadsight said. "I cannot be hurt. I will shed my skin and be born anew!"

The hyenas all leaped at once.

"No!" Shortsight gasped and tried to start forward, but Prance braced the flat of her horns against his chest and forced him back.

"There's nothing we can do," she said. "We have to run!"

Shortsight stumbled, and for a horrible moment Prance thought he might fall down, but then he broke into a clumsy, loping run, turning away from his father's fate. Prance followed after him, but she couldn't help giving a last look back.

There were hyenas with their jaws digging deep into Broadsight's legs, hyenas using their wicked claws to clamber up onto his back. He staggered but lashed out, using his long neck as a whip to toss one hyena away and into the long grass, where it let out a yelp and didn't get up again. But there were more hyenas, and they just kept coming. Broadsight's hide was running with rivulets of blood, but he was still up, until one of the hyenas managed to charge between his legs and bite down just behind one knee. He let out a furious snort and dropped to his front knees.

"She is coming," he cried out. "She will swallow you all!"

The hyenas swarmed him, biting at his neck, and Broadsight stiffened and fell.

CHAPTER FIFTEEN

"He just walked away," Chase said. She laid her head on her paws and shivered, exhausted from running up and then back down the mountain, and from telling Shadow everything that had happened. "He didn't even try to fight me, he just . . . he said Seek would be with *family*, and then he walked away."

She was lucky that Shadow was still here—first because the hyenas hadn't attacked him, and second because he hadn't left when she'd abandoned him. They hadn't talked about it, but inside, Chase was pathetically grateful. She hoped he knew it.

"How am I going to get him back?" she cried. "He's surrounded by gorillas, and snakes, and Range. . . ."

Shadow sighed. He lay down and let his muzzle rest on his own paws, mirroring Chase's. He was still weak, and there was at least one cut across his chin that she thought would always be a scar.

"Chase," he said. "You know I love Seek, too. But . . . I think he might be lost."

"No," Chase said at once. "I can't accept that, you know I can't. There has to be a way. Perhaps in the dead of night, I could . . ."

She trailed off. Shadow was simply looking at her, his black eyes deep and sad. She hated it.

She hated that he might be right.

"How can I leave him alone up there?" she said. "I know he's been . . . affected by the bite, but deep down he's probably terrified. I can't give up on him."

Shadow smiled faintly. "You don't ever give up, do you?" he said. "But you have to know that we can't fight the whole gorilla troop *and* Range. It would be madness. And it sounds like Seek is safe. For now."

"I wouldn't call it 'safe,'" Chase muttered. "But . . . I don't think they'll hurt him. Not more than they already have. He's one of them now."

"There's something else that bothers me too," Shadow said slowly. "Do you think he'd tell them how to find this den?"

Chase let out a heavy sigh and briefly tucked her nose underneath her paws. "Yes," she said. "If they asked. The snakebite changed him. And that means we should leave, I know—I know what you're about to say. But I don't know where to go! Nowhere's safe," she groaned. "And I'm *not* going too far from the gorillas. We will figure out how to get him back; we just need time."

"Right," said Shadow. He stood up and stretched, with a

soft growl of effort and a pained twitch of his tail. "I know a place where we should be safe for now. Come with me."

Chase followed him from the den, sadness hanging heavy on her shoulders. She paused to look back at the den beneath the tree, where Prowl had raised her and she had raised Seek— or tried to. Then she turned away and walked after Shadow. Without Seek, this place wasn't home anymore.

Shadow moved cautiously through the forest, stopping to sniff the air every few pawsteps, and Chase couldn't blame him. He was much brighter after the long drink from the river and the wait in the den for her to come back, but he still walked with a slight limp, and one of his eyes was not fully open. She offered to scout ahead, but not knowing where they were going, there was only so much she could do.

She did spot something as they were climbing over a series of boulders that had fallen from higher on the mountain and were now covered in slick, green moss. It was long and brown, and she almost lost her footing as she startled—but it was just a trailing vine. She nudged off the rock anyway, shuddering as she thought of the snake in the Silverback's hand, biting into Seek's paw, right where the previous bite had been. . . .

"Why?" she muttered.

"What?" Shadow had crossed the boulders and was sniffing at an exposed rocky slope on the other side.

"I just thought—why would they have the snake bite Seek a second time? He was obviously infected already. Unless it's

not permanent after all. Unless the effect is actually tempo-
rary, and if I can get him out and give him rot-meat, like the
hyena said . . ."

"Chase," Shadow said, "you can't be serious. The hyenas are
messing with you! They're trying to get you to make yourself
sick, and Seek too."

"I don't know," Chase said. "I was bitten, and I got better.
Why?"

"It could be anything," Shadow said. "*I'm* certainly not eating rot-meat on a hyena's say-so."

"Fine." Chase shrugged. "But I think I'm right about this.
The snakes have to keep biting them. Without the bites,
they'd lose their control. We have to find a way to get Seek
away from those snakes."

"We will," Shadow told her. "But first we have to rest.
Come on, it's just up here."

Chase followed Shadow up the rocky slope. It was steep
and not easy to climb. Large, jagged stones pushed up between
a scree of pebbles and brown grass, and no trees grew for a few
leopard-lengths to either side, though the ones at the edge of
the scree reached their branches over the top. It gave the place
an odd feeling—bleak but sheltered at the same time.

Shadow sniffed around one of the jagged rocks, then
twitched his tail at Chase.

"Here." And with that, he seemed to walk into the rock and
vanish. Chase scrambled after him and saw that there was a
well-hidden crack in the rock that led into a cave, about the

size of their old den, big enough for at least three leopards to curl up inside. She stepped in and immediately felt something strange on her paws.

"Is this stone . . . *warm*?" she asked. "It feels like the sun's been shining on it."

It was wonderful, actually. She padded inside and checked the cave for other entrances, or small holes something could be hiding in—the last thing she wanted was to shelter somewhere some other creature considered its home. But the only scent she found was strange—it was a sharp, mineral smell, nothing like any animal she knew. She settled down on the warm stone and gave Shadow a curious look as he lay down, weary from the climb up the slope.

"How did you know about this place?" Chase asked him.

"My mother showed it to me once," Shadow said. He paused, looking at nothing for a moment. "She used to tell me a story about why the top of the mountain is like this—why there're black rocks, like you saw with the gorillas, and why sometimes the ground is hot or it steams. Would you like to hear it?" he asked, almost shyly.

"Of course," Chase said. She settled down, tucking her paws beneath her chest.

"It started on the day when the gorillas came to the mountain," Shadow said. A cloud passed across the opening of the cave, casting them in darkness. His black fur seemed to melt into the background, leaving only his bright eyes blinking at Chase. "They were driven out of the plains, every gorilla who had ever lived, in troops of a hundred or more. They swarmed up the mountain, grabbing it for themselves with their strong paws, and they wouldn't stop. The Great Spirit saw this, and it was afraid that they would crush the mountain and drive every other creature away. So the mountain rumbled, and lightning flashed, and then the mountain threw its own rocks high into the air, to rain down on the gorillas. The rocks were hot, so hot they were aflame, and anything they touched caught fire."

He paused to give a huge yawn.

"The gorillas were driven back," he went on. "And they understood that they could live on the mountain, but they couldn't rule it. And the flaming rocks cooled down, and they became the first leopards. The Great Spirit entrusted them with the task of making sure the gorillas never climbed too high, and that's why our species have always been enemies."

"Do you think that's true?" Chase asked.

"Do I think we're actually flaming rocks?" Shadow asked wryly, putting his head down and closing his eyes.

"I mean about the Great Spirit trying to stop the gorillas." Chase laughed. "Although I don't see why we shouldn't be."

"Mmm," said Shadow. Chase waited to see if there was any more conversation coming, but the next thing she heard was a soft snore.

She smiled to herself, glad that he was getting some rest, and still amused by the idea of her ancestors being flying, fiery shards of rock.

Were we really brought here to fight against the gorillas? she wondered. She felt like that made a lot of sense. Ever since she'd known what they were, she'd been warned that they were dangerous, unpredictable. And then they'd killed Prowl.

If she was still here, she'd know what to do to rescue Seek, she thought. *Maybe she refused to join them like Range did. Maybe that's why they did it.*

Now they'd all seemingly fallen to this dark influence, the lure of *Grandmother*. . . . Chase shuddered as she thought of Range's words at the waterfall. "The Age of Sandtongue," he had called it.

But the warmth of the cave seemed to wrap around her, calming her, as if the heat of the mountain was reaching out to her.

I'm descended from fire and rock, Chase told herself, feeling determination growing in her chest as it warmed up. *And I can take on the gorillas, just like my ancestors did. I won't abandon Seek to them.*

Filled with a new energy, Chase stood up. She didn't think she could sleep right now, and she and Shadow would both need food soon. She decided to explore and see if she could find something to eat.

"I'm going hunting," she whispered to Shadow, who let out a soft breath in his sleep. But as she stepped out of the warm cave and the cool mountain air struck her again, she knew that fresh prey wasn't what she needed now. She needed rot-meat.

Her stomach turned at the idea, but she couldn't take the risk that the hyena wasn't lying. She had eaten it before and survived. She would do it again. If she was bitten and the snake-madness took her too, it would all be over for Seek.

It took a little while for her to tune her senses into looking for prey that was already dead. She ignored the rustling of leaves above her and turned away from the scent of a hare.

In the end, it was her ears who picked up her first clue—she heard growling, savage and desperate.

It was a hyena, and it was in trouble.

She snuck up into a tree and clambered closer to the sound, all her instincts telling her that this was a stupid thing to do, that even a wounded hyena would be hard to steal from. But when she got to a tree branch directly above the noises, she realized she knew this hyena. It was the same one she'd dealt with twice now. And Chase saw, with some satisfaction, that this time it was her own kind who were bothering her. Two of them, giggling as they stalked back and forth. The hyena Chase had talked to was standing over something, growling, her bristly hackles raised. It was food—and from the smell, it seemed to be rot-meat.

"What'll you give us?" one of the others said.

"I'll give you a new scar," the hyena spat. "How about that?"

Chase doubted she would be able to follow through on this threat. She was up and moving, but her leg was obviously still weak. She wouldn't give these two healthy hyenas much of a fight at all.

"We'll take the food . . . *first*," said the other. He paused to scratch behind his ear. Chase felt a pang of revulsion. So it really was true—the hyenas were willing to eat one another!

Chase couldn't let that happen. She definitely didn't owe this hyena anything, but she didn't want to see her die in this horrible way. She bunched her muscles, wiggling on the branch to make sure her balance was perfect for the leap, and then pounced, falling from the tree with her claws unsheathed and her fangs bared. She landed on one of the hyenas, bearing him to the floor, and immediately reared back and struck the other one a hard blow across the face, drawing blood.

The one who was standing immediately turned and fled into the forest with a series of hysterical yips. The one Chase had pinned wriggled and snapped at her paws, but she bent down and sank her fangs into his shoulder, then tossed him hard against a tree. He limped to his paws and backed away slowly, looking from Chase to the other hyena, and then he also vanished.

Chase watched the forest for a moment, not wanting to turn her back on them until she was sure they were gone. Then she heard heavy breathing, remembered there was still a hyena behind her, and spun on the spot.

"What was that for?" the hyena asked. "Not that I'm ungrateful." She sat down heavily, licking at her wounded leg.

"I want your rot-meat," Chase said.

"Ah. Believe me about the snakes, do you?" the hyena said. "Well, I'm flattered. And right. And you could probably kill me, so yes, you may have *a bite* of my food. You don't want any more than that," she added as Chase frowned and bared her teeth. "Delicate leopard stomachs aren't used to it."

She nudged the slab of meat toward Chase with one paw. Chase bent down to it, trying to ignore the smell. There was a greenish sheen over the top of the meat, and it felt extra slippery as she ripped off a mouthful and retreated with it. She couldn't even tell what kind of creature it had been.

At least she wasn't going to have to eat it all herself—she needed to at least try to persuade Shadow it was good for him. She had no idea how she was going to do that.

The hyena tucked in too, swallowing the rest of the nasty stuff with great gusto, and Chase turned to walk away.

Then she heard the sound of chuckling, not too far away. She looked back at the hyena. She was limping badly, and the back leg that was holding her weight was also shaking. She huffed in pain and cast a fearful look toward the noises.

Chase sighed.

"What's your name?" she asked.

"Ribsnapper," said the hyena, her eyes widening and nostrils flaring.

For a moment Chase was caught in a painful place between a shudder and a laugh. Hyenas had such ridiculous, boastful names, and yet she didn't doubt that this one had snapped a few ribs in her life.

"Well, I'm Chase," she said. "And I don't want those other hyenas to eat you, and I'm going back to somewhere safe, so . . . you can come with me, if you want. Just for the moment. Until you can actually walk on that leg."

Ribsnapper stared at her in disbelief. Which was very fair, Chase thought, because she could hardly believe she was saying this herself.

"All right," said Ribsnapper. "I will. I think I can trust that you're not about to eat me yourself, although I can't imagine why not."

"That makes two of us," Chase muttered. "Come on." She picked up the rot-meat with a small shudder, and slowly, moving at the pace of a wounded hyena, they made their way back to the rocky slope.

Shadow was awake when Chase got back, and by the time she and Ribsnapper had got inside the cave, he was pressed against the back wall and snarling.

"What are you doing?" he demanded as Chase dropped the rot-meat on the warm stone floor. "What is that hyena doing here?"

"Ribsnapper was in trouble," Chase said, trying to sound firm and brave and certain she was doing the right thing. "I said she could hide out here until she could walk normally."

"But *why*?" Shadow snapped. He sniffed at the meat and then recoiled. "I told you, I'm *not* eating that. This creature's got into your head. She's probably trying to find Seek herself so she can eat him!"

"Makes no difference to me if you eat it or not," Ribsnapper said, settling down in a warm corner of the cave and tucking her paws underneath her chest. She looked very comfortable, which seemed to make Shadow even more cross.

"Listen," Chase said, trying to sound soothing. "If there's a *chance* it might help us resist the snake curse, isn't it worth it?"

"Don't try to . . . to soothe me!" Shadow said. "I'm wounded, not stupid. Eating rot-meat, letting a hyena sleep in our den—you're turning into one of them!"

"I am not," Chase snapped back. "I'm just trying to help my

cub, any way I can. If you don't want to be involved in that, *fine.*"

"Of course I want—" Shadow began, but then he broke off. His ears twitched, and a moment later Chase heard what he'd heard. It sounded like something brushing through dry leaves, or like . . .

"Is that hissing?" Chase whispered.

She looked around and poked her head out of the cave to check for snakes swarming down the slope toward them, but there were no snakes anywhere.

But still the hissing went on, and when Chase pulled back inside, she realized the sound was coming from *underneath* her. She looked down, treading nervously with her paws on the warm stone.

"I saw steam coming out of the stone when I saw the gorillas," Chase said. "Maybe it's something like that?"

Shadow shook his head in utter bewilderment and started sniffing around the edges of the cave that Chase had just checked. The hissing was growing fainter now, and after a few more moments it was gone.

Chase glanced at Ribsnapper and was startled to see the hyena's expression had completely changed. From her smugly comfortable position taking up a good portion of the warm floor, she had backed up until she was pressed into the corner of the cave. Her eyes were wide with fright, and her ears pulled back.

"It's not the steam," she whispered.

"Then what is it?" Shadow demanded.

Ribsnapper hesitated. "I only know what those who are taken by the snake-curse call it," she said.

"And what's that?" Chase asked.

Ribsnapper looked down at the ground, as if she could see right through it to the source of the terrible sound.

"They call it *Grandmother*."

CHAPTER SIXTEEN

Spider gave up on speaking grasstongue and switched to a series of incomprehensible snorts and bellows, but the crocodile kept coming. Did he even really speak sandtongue? Bramble had no idea. Panic gripped him, and he fumbled along the walls, trying to back away.

"Not this way!" Moonflower yelped. Bramble tried to turn, bumped his elbow on the tunnel, and managed to crane his neck around in time to see Moonflower rush up next to him, a jaw full of snapping teeth right on her heels.

"More crocodiles!" Bramble said. "Spider, what do we do?"

Spider was still grunting and hissing, his voice rising in increasing panic. Moonflower grabbed on to Bramble's hand, and he thought, *This is it. This is how we die. The message never reaches Great Father, the evil spreads from the mountain, and all good things in Bravelands come to an end. . . .*

But Moonflower lifted his hand and pressed it to the tunnel wall, dragging it back across the stone until it met empty air.

"Feel it?"

It was another tunnel, a gap in the wall that Bramble had completely missed before.

"Got it, go!" Bramble said. Moonflower slipped into the opening, and the crocodile's jaws snapped shut right where her feet had been. Bramble grabbed Spider and dragged him into the new tunnel.

"I don't know what's happening to them!" Spider said. He sounded upset, but at least when Bramble let go of him he didn't stop moving. The three of them half ran, half crawled through the darkness, passing through patches of pale gray light and other spots where the dark was total, and Bramble knew he could be running headlong into the mouth of a crocodile and he wouldn't know it. He heard Spider's scampering footsteps behind him, and then the stomping and slithering of the crocodiles.

Moonflower cursed up ahead, and he almost ran right into her.

"Dead end!" she cried.

The space widened out, so Bramble and Spider could squeeze in beside Moonflower, but though Bramble ran his hands over every bit of wall he could reach, she was right—there was no way out.

"Try to dig!" Spider said.

Bramble and Moonflower turned and started to scrabble at

the earth, but it was dry and hardened. The plodding of the crocodiles was getting louder and louder, and they were making a hissing sound now too, one that reminded Bramble horribly of the sound that had filled the clearing when he'd witnessed the gorillas allowing themselves to be bitten by snakes.

In his horror and panic, he turned and punched the earth, pounding it, hoping it would loosen. His knuckles stung, and the earth didn't move. Moonflower joined him, slamming her fists against the tunnel wall, until suddenly a sprinkling of earth fell down, right on top of Bramble's head. He looked up and found himself squinting through a long crack in the ceiling. On the other side, daylight glimmered.

"Keep hitting it!" Spider gasped, and all three of them pounded on the earth until the crack widened. The earth began to fall like rain, getting in Bramble's eyes. "Now climb!" Spider said and scurried up the wall. Moonflower followed him, and Bramble brought up the rear, trying to keep half an eye on the tunnel. As the ceiling fell in and light burst into the little cave, he saw a green, scaly nose poke from the tunnel. Then a shower of mud slipped down, covering it, and he heard an angry hissing.

Moonflower and Spider reached down, and Bramble grabbed their hands and dragged himself out of the thing that had once been a cave but was now more like a pit in the ground, full of loose earth. Once he was out, he rolled away from the edge as Moonflower worked around the perimeter of the pit, thumping the earth until everything that was going to fall in seemed to have done so. When she was done, she sat down hard and shook herself violently, dislodging mud, dust, and a few cobwebs.

"The crocodiles won't come up this way," Spider said, looking down at the pile of earth where the entrance to the tunnel had been. "Too messy. Too dry. They'll go back to the tunnels where it's nice and damp."

He sounded sad.

Bramble scratched at his head and shoulders, brushing off the loose earth. He looked around them and then breathed a huge sigh of relief.

"At least we made it," he said. On one side of them, a little way away, the river sparkled under the noonday sun. On the other side, and closer, was the edge of the forest.

"That's right!" said Spider, brightening. "I told you I could get you across the river."

Moonflower glared at him, red-eyed and furious, and Bramble was briefly afraid she might try to wring his neck.

"We almost died!" he said. "You said the crocodiles were your friends!"

"They were," Spider said. He looked down at his long fingers, picking at their nails. "Something's changed. Something's wrong. They didn't even respond when I spoke sandtongue to them."

"Maybe there's a reason for that," Moonflower said. "*Sandtongue*. Just like the snakes that bit Burbark and the rest of the troop. Just like that lizard that pulled you into the water, Bramble. And just like that *thing* that took my mother," she added quietly.

"Trouble with the sandtongues?" Spider scratched his chin, which spread mud over his feet. "That is worrying. And something to tell Great Father Thorn, for sure. Let's go quickly. He'll know what to do."

The forest was a strange place, much like every place they'd been on the plains so far. It was very flat at first, and even when the landscape changed it was barely enough to break a gorilla's stride. The trees gathered closer together, the farther inside they went, but the ground was never as dark or as sheltered as the mountain. The whole place felt drier, which seemed to Bramble to make no sense, with this many trees growing this close to a river. But they were different trees, too, their trunks generally both shorter and thinner, some of them bending and twisting like the ones they'd rested in on the plain. Different-colored flowers and leaves sprung from bushes around their roots, but there were few dripping vines, and the ones there were had a brownish look to them, as if they'd snap if he tried to climb on them.

Bramble's stomach rumbled. "Is there anything to eat in this forest?" he asked Spider.

Spider let out a barking laugh. "Is there anything to eat? Oh, you poor monkey. You two keep walking that way, I'll be back," he said, pointing a long finger in the direction he'd been leading them, and then springing up into the branches of a tree and disappearing.

"I'll bet you a handful of nuts he never comes back," Moonflower muttered.

But she was wrong—they hadn't been walking alone for very long before Spider dropped out of a tree in front of them, holding an armful of fruit. Bramble recognized lychees, a mango, and a big round fruit he'd never seen before. Spider handed them over, and the gorillas tucked in gratefully. Bramble discovered that the strange fruit had a thin rind, underneath which was a beautifully juicy segmented fruit. Spider explained that it was called an orange.

After their feast, they journeyed on until they came to a grassy clearing, full of old, moss-covered tree stumps. It looked like a lot of trees had fallen or been torn down in this place, many years ago. At one end, there was a large boulder, taller than either of the gorillas.

"Here we are," said Spider cheerfully. "The Great Father's clearing. Thorn? Thorn! Visitors!" He walked into the center of the clearing, cupping his mouth to make his hooting call carry farther.

For a moment, nothing happened. Then, all at once, more baboons dropped from the trees all around Bramble and Moonflower. Four of them, each younger and larger than Spider. They stared at the gorillas, eyeing them with curiosity. Bramble stared back.

"What are you," one of them demanded, "and what's your business here?"

"I'm a gorilla," Bramble said. "I'm here to see the Great Father."

"A gorilla!" one of the baboons cackled, and Bramble's heart sank.

"Don't tell me—gorillas aren't real," Moonflower muttered, rolling her eyes at Bramble.

"Gorillas!" said another baboon, leaning on a stick, apparently weak from how hilarious this was.

"I suppose you came down from the mountain, did you?" said a third. "Is that why your heads look like big weird rocks?"

"What do you mean, *weird rocks?*" Bramble said, raising his hands to feel his head.

The baboon with the stick reached out and poked him in the leg with it—quite gently, but firmly. "He *feels* real," she said and then collapsed in laughter again.

Another one leaned in and sniffed at Bramble. "Smells real, too! Phew." He backed away with his hand over his nose.

Bramble had had enough of this. He planted his feet and stood up, spreading his chest like he'd seen Burbark and Cassava do, until he was towering over the closest baboon. He thumped his chest and gave a loud bark. The thump actually hurt more than he'd expected, but it had the effect he'd been hoping for—the baboons gibbered and backed off slightly.

"These *are* gorillas," Spider said calmly, standing next to the baboon with the stick and looking up at Bramble with approval. "And they *did* come from the mountain. What about you, Cricket Highleaf? Where did you come from? Why aren't you four with your own troop?"

"The Great Father needs our protection," said Cricket.

Behind her, Bramble saw one of the other baboons nod and try to puff his chest out, just like Bramble had done.

"Cashew Crownleaf herself picked us to come and guard him," he said.

"What about Thorn's lion friend?"

"Gallant's not here," said another baboon. "He's gone off with Moth. They're looking for a gazelle who's vanished. Something about not having a shadow."

Bramble looked at Moonflower, in case she was following any of this, but she looked just as blank as he felt. Spider scratched his head and then nodded.

"Well, he'll be all right if he's with Moth," he said.

"I'm confused," Bramble put in. "Is the Great Father here or not? We need to speak with him urgently!"

"You look like you're confused a lot," said one of the baboons under his breath.

"Hey!" Bramble barked. "We've come a long way to be here! All the way from the mountain! And we *must* see Great Father Thorn. We have a vital message for him."

"Oh yeah?" said Cricket. "Let's hear it then."

Bramble looked at Moonflower, who nodded. He took a deep breath.

"The message is: *evil spreads from the mountain, unless wisdom stands in its path.*"

The baboons looked at one another.

"That's it?" said Cricket.

One of the other baboons sniggered, and then all of them were laughing again.

Bramble felt like a fruit that someone had squeezed all the juice out of. He deflated, sitting down hard in the grass, embarrassment and anger heating his cheeks.

So much for our important message. We came all the way here, but they won't even listen.

Moonflower was stepping forward, frowning as if she was about to take the baboons to task, when yet another baboon emerged from behind the big boulder. This one was old, like Spider—even older, Bramble thought, and definitely frailer. He made his way across the clearing at a limping run. The others turned and saw him approaching, and their laughter died down.

Is this him? Bramble thought. *Has he come to tell us our message is stupid, too?*

"Hello, Mud," said Spider. "How are you?"

The baboon called Mud walked up to Bramble and looked from him to Moonflower, squinting with one good eye and one milky and unfocused.

"Two black boulders roll down from the mountain," he muttered.

"Um . . . sorry?" Bramble said.

"Forgive me," Mud said. "Something I heard recently. My name is Mud, and I am the Great Father's Starleaf. That means I know a little more about the Great Spirit's messages than these . . . baboons," he finished, glaring at the four guards as if he had wanted to call them something rather stronger. "Both of you, come with me."

He turned and headed back toward the boulder. Bramble moved to follow him, giving Cricket Highleaf a pointed look on the way past.

"I'll stay here," said Spider cheerfully.

Mud the elderly Starleaf led Bramble and Moonflower around the side of the boulder to a sheltered spot where a large bush had grown up one side of the rock and a space had been hollowed out underneath. Bramble recognized it as a den, even before he saw the baboon sitting inside.

"I must warn you," said Mud with a sigh. "Great Father Thorn is . . . probably not quite what you two were expecting."

He held back a branch and allowed Bramble to duck under the bush. There was enough room for both him and Moonflower to get inside with the Great Father, but not for Mud to join them.

Thorn was sitting with his back against the boulder. His eyes were downcast, and mistier than Mud's. He held a stick in his hand, and as Bramble watched, he drew patterns in the dirt in front of him. Swirls and wavy lines, some with sharp, jutting angles, many that just seemed to curl in on themselves forever. He didn't look up as the gorillas entered his den, and he didn't speak.

"Thorn," Mud said. "These two gorillas have come to deliver a message from the mountain."

The elderly baboon did not look up, but he did begin to speak.

"Everywhere," he muttered, in a voice that rasped in his throat. "From here to there, there to here. Too late, too late to choose, oh dear."

Bramble slowly turned to look at Moonflower, whose face was a picture of incredulity that mirrored his own.

They'd come all this way, through drought and rivers and tunnels full of crocodiles, to bring their message . . . to this creature?

For a moment, Thorn's movements sped up, the drawing in the mud became agitated, and he rocked back and forth against the boulder.

"Never," he slurred. "Never ever, no. Shadows and stars, no! Ha!" Then he slumped back against the stone, and his drawing turned sluggish again. "Berry . . . ?" he whispered.

"That's enough, I think," Mud said, laying a gentle hand on Moonflower's arm. Bramble agreed with him. It was plenty.

They retreated from the den, and Mud sat down on a patch of moss, fiddling with a pile of polished stones beside him.

"As you can see," he said, "the Great Father is in no state to receive or understand your message. He is sick. We've done what we can for him, but it seems . . . it seems he has lost his mind."

"Did something happen to him?" Moonflower asked.

"He was bitten," Mud said. "By a snake."

Bramble let out a sigh of deep despair.

"A snakebite," he said. "Then he's right. It's too late." He looked at Moonflower, an ache of horror in his heart. "We were too late."

CHAPTER SEVENTEEN

Prance and Shortsight trudged through the long grass in silence. They had managed to slip away while the hyenas were . . . busy.

I have to get Shortsight back to his herd, Prance thought. *The poor thing has nobody now.*

But he does have me.

She glanced up at Shortsight's face every once in a while, hoping that if he needed something she would know. But the foal was almost expressionless, staring at the ground ahead of him.

It wasn't too hard to follow the giraffe herd's trail, but they had managed to get far enough ahead that Prance couldn't see them. Every time they passed a tree or a large rock, she hoped they would appear in the distance, but so far they never had.

Broadsight's words kept repeating in her head. *I will do my mistress's bidding until the end. I cannot be hurt. I will shed my skin and be born anew.*

What did that mean?

She had to get back to the Great Father and tell him about it—or tell Mud and Moth, if Thorn wasn't well enough to understand. The sandtongues were the key to all of this, she was certain—didn't snakes shed their skin? Could it be that the giraffe had started to think he *was* a snake?

That didn't make any sense, but none of this did.

First, get Shortsight to his herd, she told herself. *I can do that.*

The giraffes' trail led them to a small watering hole, where the mud of the bank was churned up with hoofprints. The herd had stopped to drink here recently, so Prance and Shortsight must be gaining on them.

Prance scanned the watering hole for predators, but she didn't spot any obvious crocodiles lurking under the surface—perhaps it was too small for them anyway. The giraffes had moved on, but there were three other animals standing on the bank, drinking together. A zebra, a tiny dik-dik, and an elderly-looking wildebeest.

Strange, Prance thought as she walked down to the edge of the water. *Three herd animals, but no herds.*

Was this another one of those strange occurrences? Were the sandtongues somehow behind this too? Had they been lost, or expelled from their own herds? Perhaps they were going through something like what she'd been through. They certainly made an odd sight, with the lone gazelle and giraffe joining the three herdless creatures on the bank.

"Good afternoon," she said politely to the wildebeest, who was drinking beside her, as Shortsight bent his tall neck to lower his head to the watering hole.

The wildebeest didn't answer.

"Hello," said the zebra.

"My friend Shortsight has lost his family, and I'm helping him find them," Prance said, half hoping that volunteering their situation would lead one of the others to do the same. "Have you seen a herd of giraffes pass by?"

The three creatures looked at one another, and the wildebeest gave a heavy sigh and shook his head. Shortsight looked up, frowning with worry.

"No, haven't seen them," said the dik-dik.

"Well, their hoofprints clearly lead here—" Prance began. She'd been about to concede that the three animals could have missed them, but the dik-dik interrupted her.

"What're you saying? We're not lying. No giraffes," she squeaked, her long nose quivering nervously.

All right, this is very strange, Prance thought. She bent down, intending to ask the dik-dik if she was feeling all right and take a look to see if she could spot any snakebites at the same time. But as she did, the wildebeest put down its head and stumbled right into her, pressing the side of his head to her horns.

"What—" Prance muttered.

"Run," whispered the wildebeest. "You're in danger. Get

the foal out of here, before its's too late."

Prance drew herself up in shock. She stared at the wilde-beest for a moment, then gave him a tiny, thankful nod.

"Come on, Shortsight," she said. "We should go. We can catch your herd if we hurry."

"N-no," the dik-dik said. "Stay, there's plenty of water! There's no more for miles. You'll regret it if you leave now."

Prance saw the zebra squeeze his eyes closed and snort through his nostrils, as if he didn't want to know what was going on.

"No, I think we'll go," she said, backing away from the three creatures. She gave one more apprehensive glance at the surface of the water, and then she turned around to trot back up the bank and saw the lion.

She let out a panicked gasp. That wasn't Gallant. It was thinner and smaller, a lioness with no mane and scrawny-looking shoulders, creeping through the grass, crouched to spring. Prance backed up, scanning the grass. Which way could they run?

But it wasn't just one lion. All around her, more of the stalking shapes appeared, closing in from every direction.

"Lions!" she managed to gasp. "Shortsight! Get ready to run when I tell you!"

They couldn't just run and take their chances—she'd have to wait for one of the lions to spring and try to get out through the gap they left in the closing circle. But Shortsight's clumsy foal legs made him a target and a liability. He stumbled and slipped on the mud as he backed away from the lions. She couldn't just leave him. She looked at the other three herdless creatures, but none of them had raised their heads to look when she'd called out. The wildebeest's eyes flicked to hers, and he gave another heavy sigh.

"Sorry," said the zebra in a small voice. "She made us do it."

The lions rose from the grass, closing in slowly, which was somehow worse than if they'd charged.

I could still make it, Prance thought desperately, the smell of the predators sparking the same sense of nervy energy that had always washed over her when the Us said *run*. She could probably slip between them, leap the bushes on the bank, and at least she'd have a chance—but Shortsight wouldn't make it. She'd be sacrificing him for herself, and it wasn't his time, any more than it was hers. So she stood her ground and tried to stare down the lioness who stepped out of the long grass. . . .

Wait. I know her, Prance thought.

The lioness walked with a limp, though the weak leg didn't seem to hurt her much or slow her down. Her face was scarred, and as she peeled back her lips to growl at Prance and Shortsight, Prance saw that one of her teeth was chipped.

This was the lioness who had tried to catch Prance, back when she was with the herd, when she lost the Us, and her shadow. Prance had kicked her in the face. Now Prance watched her approach with a terror in her heart that she hadn't felt in days.

This is the lion who was supposed to kill me. Is she here to finally do it?

"Good work," said the lioness. "You've earned a few more days of life."

Prance realized, in horror, that she was talking to the three herdless animals. They all turned around, the zebra and the wildebeest hanging their heads, not meeting Prance's gaze. But the little dik-dik marched forward, as bold as an elephant, and raised her tiny muzzle to whisper into the lioness's ear.

The lioness listened, and then her eyes narrowed and flashed as she looked up and fixed her gaze on the wildebeest.

"I cannot abide disloyalty," she snarled. "You haven't been disloyal to me, have you, Dustback?"

Dustback the wildebeest met her gaze, then to Prance's shock, he fell to his front knees.

"I am sorry, Menace," he said. "A lapse of judgment. The giraffe is so young. Please . . . have mercy on me. I am old and weak."

Menace sat back on her haunches and gazed down at Dustback, her lip curling in disgust.

"Very well," she said. "You may go."

Dustback's head shot up and his eyes widened. "Go?" he said, his voice cracking. "You—you're letting me *go*?"

"You said yourself, you're old and weak. If you're going to keep trying to *starve* my pride, I don't need you. *Go*."

Dustback got up, and the lions parted to let him pass. The wildebeest threw a terrified, apologetic glance back at Prance and Shortsight, but started to lumber away through the grass, looking back in worry every few steps.

Prance longed to sprint through the gap before it closed, but she couldn't leave Shortsight, and she didn't want to do anything to endanger Dustback's escape, either. He might have been part of this horrible trap, but at least he had tried to help her.

"So you use lone herd animals as bait," she said to Menace, the shake in her voice giving away her fear, even though she tried to sound confident. "To make your prey think it's safe. Is that right?"

"Are you going to eat us?" Shortsight quavered, backing away until his rear legs were submerged up to the knees in the watering hole.

"No, I don't think I will," said Menace. "After all, I've just had to let one of my pride go. You two will join Flick and Gloomfriend, and you *will* fulfill your role—which, yes, is as bait for other stupid grass-eaters."

Prance gave a violent shudder. This was evil—inventively, creatively evil.

"You will follow my orders, or you will die. I don't tolerate disloyalty."

She snarled and tossed her head, and three of the other lions peeled off from the circle and started to run, charging down Dustback. He turned, saw them, and broke into a panicked sprint, but he was old and they were fast. He veered around a nearby bush, the lions skidding in the dry earth as they spun to follow him. A moment later, there was a crash, a roar, and a soft groan, then silence.

"Do I make myself clear?" said Menace, without turning

her head to watch, as the rest of the pride closed in on Prance and Shortsight.

"Perfectly," said Prance.

A blood-red sunset was fading on the western edge of the sky, leaving vivid blue and deep black above, sprinkled with stars. Prance sat in the grass with Shortsight, Flick, and Gloomfriend, surrounded by sated, dozing lions. Some of them snored and twitched their paws, others licked the blood from their lips and watched the four bait creatures through heavy-lidded eyes.

There were eight, including Menace. Prance doubted they would ever be left entirely unobserved, but even if every one of the lions fell asleep, they were curled up close enough that stepping over one without waking them would be impossible.

It was an odd sort of pride. For a start, there were several males, but no male pride leader—Menace was obviously in charge—and the rest were a motley collection of young and old, many of them bearing scars. One had no tail, another only one ear. The one closest to Prance slobbered massively in her sleep and had a missing fang.

"It's not such a bad life, working for Menace," Flick said through a mouthful of grass. "Just don't get soft like Dustback did, and you'll be all right."

Prance threw a disgusted look at the little dik-dik. She could understand following Menace's orders if they had no choice. But how could Flick accept it so readily, and much worse, turn one of her fellow bait creatures over to Menace without even being asked? Some creatures would do anything for a sense of safety, but Prance knew in her bones that one day Menace would turn on Flick, and then no amount of sucking up would save her.

She didn't say any of this aloud. As much as she hated it, she had her own reasons for wanting Menace to think she was cooperating.

"Shortsight," she said. "I need to do something. You should stay here and do whatever Menace says . . . for now," she added in a whisper.

Then she stood up and slowly walked over to Menace. She did everything she could to look unthreatening and calm, and not to give the impression she was trying to run away.

"Menace, may I speak with you?" she asked.

Menace was picking at her teeth with one claw and narrowed her eyes at Prance as she approached. "How polite. Yes, why not? What would you like to say to me?"

Prance took a deep breath. "I know you're probably expecting me to beg for my life," she began.

"Not really," Menace said. "Most don't bother."

"Well, I have a duty to ask you to let me go. But not for my own sake. For all of Bravelands."

"Oh, this is good. Go on, why are you so important, herdless one?" Menace sat up on her haunches, her tail twitching in amusement.

"I've discovered a threat to Bravelands," Prance said. "Some sort of sandtongue . . . conspiracy, or sickness, I'm not sure. But it's all over the plains, and it's getting worse. I was sent out here alone to investigate it, and I must be allowed passage to return to the Great Father and tell him what I've found. If I don't get back to him soon, every grasstongue and skytongue creature may be at risk, including you and your pride. It's in your interest to let me go."

She waited, holding her breath.

Menace snorted. "The *Great Father*? That jumped-up little monkey? Is he still alive?"

I hope so, Prance thought.

"Let me tell you something, gazelle. Lions don't follow the Great Father—*real* ones don't, anyway," Menace said, her amusement fading. She leaned her muzzle close to Prance and snarled. "My father was a *true* lion, the rightful ruler of this land by might and conquest. Your Great Spirit was almost his, until the monkey tricked him. I'm not afraid of snakes, and I will never help the so-called Great Father with anything. So sit down, before I decide your loyalties are too confused for this pride."

"Your father was Titan?" Prance asked.

Menace growled, and Prance hurried back to Shortsight's side and sat down in the grass.

"And don't you ever forget it," piped up the lion to Menace's left. Prance didn't have much practice at guessing the age of lions, but if he was an adult he was a very young one. She'd noticed him before, as Menace force-walked her new pride members to this place. His mane was starting to come in, but mostly growing up from the top of his head and in messy patches on his neck. He was the least scarred of any

of Menacepride. He was tall and skinny, in a way that sug-
gested he would be a powerful lion one day, if he could ever
get enough to eat. "Menace, didn't you say Titan killed a crocodile once?"

Menace seemed to relax. She settled back on her stomach,
a pleased look on her face.

"*Once?*" she chuckled. "Terror, you should know better.
Titan used to swim in crocodile-infested waters, just for fun.
Titan killed crocodiles with ease. He ripped out their leaders'
hearts and consumed their spirits. Basks ran when they saw
him coming."

Prance caught one of the other lions, an elder male who
had been snoozing, look over at Menace and roll his eyes.

It soon became clear that Titan was Menace's favorite
topic, closely followed by how Titan had been betrayed and
his rightful conquest of Bravelands stolen from him. Prance
listened to her stories of her father's terrible deeds in horrified fascination. She had never met a creature who gloried in
destruction like Menace did. She had only heard Titan's name
whispered, in stories intended to frighten young gazelles into
being careful at the watering hole and listening to the Us.
Menace seemingly had no interest at all in making him sound
like he was actually good, or noble. According to Menace, he
was the most evil creature ever to walk the plains, and the idea
seemed to delight her.

Eventually, after telling several horrible stories with violent
endings—and sometimes violent beginnings and middles—
Menacepride slipped toward slumber.

"Should we try to go?" Shortsight asked in a quavering voice, barely above the sound of the breeze in the grass around them.

"No," Prance said. "They'll hurt you. Just get some sleep, Shortsight. I will find a way to get you back to your herd."

Shortsight nodded and tucked his head around to rest on his haunches, closing his eyes. Gloomfriend was already asleep, as was Flick, her nose shuddering with every breath.

But Prance couldn't sleep. She sat still, alone in the circle of sleeping creatures, her horns pointed to the stars. For a moment, she felt like the only waking creature in the world. An eerie calm came over her.

I must escape, she thought. *I must find a way to get word to Gallant and the others. Gallant will get me back to Thorn. . . . I just hope I'm not too late.*

She looked down, just as the moon emerged from behind a cloud, and the shadow of her horns was cast on the ground in front of her.

Wait . . . my shadow! It's back!

She sprang to her hooves and took a step, and she saw the shadow move too. Then a strange, prickly feeling made her turn to look behind her.

She was still lying down. At least, a gazelle body that looked just like hers was sitting where she had been, its head bowed and eyes closed in what looked like sleep.

I'm doing it again, she thought. *Whatever I did before, when I overheard Mud talking about his vision. I'm doing it right now!*

She still had no idea how, or why, but now was not the time

to stand around trying to figure it out.

Trust the Great Spirit. Trust my shadow-self. And go!

She leaped gracefully over the sleeping body of Terror and landed on the other side on hooves made of shadow, silent and invisible.

With a last look back at her sleeping body and Shortsight curled up next to her, she broke into a run. The grass didn't so much as bend under her hooves, but the plains around her began to blur as she ran faster and faster, hopping this way and that to avoid trees and rocks, leaping over streams. The stars above seemed to shine brighter, lighting her way. As quick as the wind, quicker than any gazelle had ever run before, she followed her instincts toward the Great Father's forest. She didn't need to slow to check her path. She let her heart lead her, and it wasn't long before she saw the moonlit forest canopy glowing darkly on the horizon.

"Prance . . . ?" came a voice, distant but close at the same time. Prance veered toward it and slowed gradually to a weightless walk as she saw the shape of a lion with a baboon on his back, walking across the dark plains.

"What? Do you see her?" Gallant said, stopping and twisting his head to peer into the darkness.

"I . . . I thought I did," Moth said. "Prance? Are you there?"

Prance stepped up to them. "I'm here, Moth!" she said. "You saw me before. See me now."

Moth was looking around, her eyes seeming to skim over Prance, as if part of her didn't want to see her.

Prance steeled herself and concentrated. "Moth, Gallant. I'm here."

Both her friends jumped, and Moth's hands clenched in Gallant's mane.

"I heard that," Gallant said, awe in his voice. "Prance, where *are* you?"

"I think . . . I think this has happened before!" Moth gasped. "What's going on?"

"There's no time to explain," Prance said. *And I can't, anyway,* she thought, suppressing a slightly hysterical chuckle. "I need your help."

CHAPTER EIGHTEEN

Chase stared up at the dark sky. Somewhere up there, she knew, Prowl was running among the stars, doing whatever leopard spirits did—perhaps there were forests full of delicious prey, or perhaps a soft, warm den where she could lie all day without a care in the world.

She hoped that if Prowl was looking down at Bravelands, she could see that Chase was doing her best.

I will get him back, she thought. *If I have to battle every gorilla and befriend every hyena in the forest to do it.*

"Hey," said a soft voice, and Shadow emerged from the darkness of the cave. He sat down beside her, and then bent his head and brushed his cheek against her shoulder. Chase let out a soft sound of surprise, but then leaned over and nudged him back. "It's my turn to keep watch," Shadow said, his voice rumbling against Chase's fur.

"You're not completely recovered," she said. "I can take the night watch, if you want."

"I feel much better. And you need rest too," Shadow reminded her. "Anyway, it's your turn to lie next to the stinky hyena."

Chase sighed. "I don't know if I can get to sleep."

"Still thinking about Seek?"

"What is he doing now? Does he have somewhere warm and safe to sleep? Are they going to hurt him? Are they going to make him do something terrible?" Chase shook her head. "I'm sorry, I'm just not ready to give up on him."

"I know," said Shadow. "But I don't want to lose you too."

Chase gently leaned her forehead against the side of Shadow's neck.

"Go on," he said. "Get inside and get some sleep."

"All right," Chase said. "But just till dawn, then we can switch back."

"We'll see," said Shadow.

Chase slinked past him, back inside the cave.

She felt a small shudder as she stepped onto the stone floor, warm from the vents below, and remembered the sound, and the name Ribsnapper had given it. *Grandmother.* She already knew that if Grandmother was a real creature, she never wanted to meet her.

The spot where Shadow had been was even warmer, and it smelled pleasantly familiar, even if the hyena's scent was also filling the space.

As Chase flopped down, Ribsnapper opened one eye.

"So is the little one his cub?" she said.

"What? No, he's not my mate!" Chase whispered, curling her tail with embarrassment and hoping Shadow couldn't hear them.

"Why not? You obviously like him."

Chase sniffed. "I do not."

The hyena just stared at her for a moment. "Uh-huh. Well. He likes you. So what's the problem?"

"You don't know what you're talking about. It's not that simple," Chase said.

"It would be if you were hyenas," Ribsnapper chuckled. "I remember, with my first mate—"

"Well we're *not*," Chase interrupted. She didn't want to hear whatever story Ribsnapper was about to tell. "I may be willing to let you share our cave, but I'm not taking hyena advice on romance."

"Just on eating rot-meat?" said Ribsnapper slyly.

Chase curled up, tucked her head under her paws, and let her tail fall over her head, but she couldn't block out the sound of the hyena giggling to herself in the darkness.

The next time Chase awoke, the mouth of the cave was visible, but dark gray. It must be before dawn. She got up, stretched, and padded out to the rocky slope to sniff the air.

The mountainside was shrouded in thick mist, and there was no sign of Shadow.

"*Shadow?*" Chase hissed. "Are you out here?"

The mist was thick and opaque, the kind that felt as if a

cloud had fallen from the sky and settled over the mountain. It was almost darker out there now than it had been in the depths of the night when the stars had been out.

Chase scanned the small area she could make out, and her heart began to race.

"Shadow!" she called, louder this time. But there was no sign of him and no answer. She sniffed the ground and found his scent. He'd been here. Recently. But then he'd left. . . .

"What's happening?" Ribsnapper said, emerging from the cave and yawning hugely.

"Shadow's gone," Chase said.

Ribsnapper scented the air and then sniffed at the ground. "No blood," she said. "And we'd have heard a struggle. Looks like he wandered off. Probably just gone to hunt."

"He's in no condition to hunt," Chase snapped. "If he has, he's an idiot who might get himself hurt." *And I don't think that's where he's gone*, she added to herself. "Come on, we have to go after him."

She expected Ribsnapper to argue that what she had to do was stay in the warm cave while Chase raced off after Shadow, but the hyena yawned again and stretched, then blinked coolly at Chase.

"Well, lead the way then," she said.

Chase put her nose down and sniffed out Shadow's scent, and they started out, scrambling up to the very top of the rocky slope. The mist closed behind them and opened in front of them barely a few leopard-lengths at a time, and Chase couldn't see where they were headed at first—but her instincts turned more and more into certainties as they entered a forested area and followed Shadow's trail until another scent crossed it.

Gorillas.

"He's gone to get the cub back," Ribsnapper said. Chase was glad she hadn't had to say it. "I thought you said it wasn't his?"

"It's not. It's complicated," Chase muttered. "What is he *thinking*? He's not strong enough to try to sneak him out alone—what if Range spots him? What if he wakes up the gorillas? He'll be killed!"

I don't want to lose you too, Shadow had said. Chase hung her head. Maybe he was trying to tell her that he'd rather risk it himself, in his own stupid way. Maybe he was trying to tell her not to follow him.

Well, whatever you were trying to say, I won't let you go in there alone, she thought. The mist lay less thick as they pressed farther into the forest, and the sky began to lighten just a little. The sun was still a little way off from rising, but at least Chase could see the tree trunks in front of her now. She still heard the sound of the gorillas before she saw them. They were snoring.

"I'm going up," she whispered to Ribsnapper, nodding to a low branch that would lead her up into a tree that overhung the gorillas' nests.

"Don't fall," the hyena whispered back.

Chase leaped into the tree, moving as fluidly, treading as lightly as she could. She snuck out onto a branch, ducking past a spray of leaves, and jumped as the branch trembled. She crouched back and peered into the gloom, afraid she'd walked right into a gorilla's nest, and looked up into the black face of Shadow.

He blinked at her, his ears flicking with worry.

"Do you see him?" Chase whispered. This was no time for them to argue about who left who behind, or who should be resting more. Shadow seemed to agree. He gave a brief nod and gingerly walked along the branch, to point his gaze into the heart of the gorilla nests below. She followed him and looked down, her heart in her mouth.

There was Seek, the little bundle of mottled yellow and brown fur, his belly rising and falling in slumber. He looked as sweet as he had done when he'd slept in Chase's den, before any of this had happened—except that he was curled up in the crook of the Silverback's arm. The huge gorilla was asleep on his back in a pile of crushed green leaves, his arms and legs spread carelessly wide, snoring like the sound of stones rattling down the mountainside. And Seek was curled up next to him, looking as comfortable as if he'd been with his own mother. Chase dug her claws into the tree branch in horror and revulsion.

"No sign of Range," Shadow whispered. "Maybe hunting."

"Ribsnapper's waiting down below," Chase whispered back. Shadow shot her a surprised look. "I know. But she's come this far. Maybe she'll help?"

Shadow's expression of surprise turned to doubt, but he followed Chase in silence as they slipped back to the tree trunk and then scrambled down it, as silently as they possibly could.

"The Silverback?" Ribsnapper muttered when they'd retreated a little way back so they could talk. "Well, there's no sneaking him out from there."

Shadow looked angry, and Chase thought he was about to snap at the hyena for her unhelpful words, when Ribsnapper spoke again.

"I'll cause a distraction," she said. "While the gorillas are confused and all looking at me, you run in and snatch the cub."

"Why?" Shadow asked. "Why would you help us? Why should we trust you?"

Ribsnapper let out a small, suppressed chuckle. "You're supposedly the great hunters. Don't you smell it? The sand-tongue curse. It's all over this place. We might not be the most trustworthy, but right now, I hate the snakes more than I hate you. Once this is over, we can go back to being enemies, but if I can hold up their Grandmother's plans in any way, I will. Does that satisfy you?"

Shadow hesitated and then nodded.

"Good. Get as close as you can. You'll know when it's time."

And with a last nod to Chase, Ribsnapper loped away into the undergrowth.

The two leopards pressed as close as they could to the gorilla nests, slinking beneath bushes and over rocks, until they were lying on their bellies behind a tree, less than a leopard-length from a snoring gorilla. She snuffled and turned over in her sleep, and Chase pressed her shoulder to Shadow's, steadying both of them.

From here she could see the path she would take to the

Silverback's nest. As long as the gorilla on the other side of the tree got up to follow Ribsnapper's distraction, and one more either did the same or stayed fast asleep in a hollow of a tree a little farther up the slope, then she would have a clear run to the nest.

And if the Silverback picks up Seek, or wakes up but stays to guard him?

Well, that's why it's better there are two of us.

They'd agreed, before they'd gotten any closer. The one who got to Seek first would grab him and run as fast as they could. No looking back, no staying to fight. And the other . . .

The other would try to follow, but if they couldn't, they would buy time.

Chase pressed her forehead to the side of Shadow's face again and twined her tail with his, just for a moment. Shadow let out a tiny sigh and leaned into her. Perhaps Ribsnapper wasn't completely making things up. . . .

Just then a howling shriek split the air, and Chase startled and pulled apart from Shadow.

It's happening.

The sound of a hyena, cackling in hysterical triumph, echoed around the forest. It was a sound that made Chase's skin crawl, and the gorillas clearly felt the same. They started awake and let out groans and grunts of confusion and anger. The one in the nest right beside Chase and Shadow balled her fist and thumped the ground.

The Silverback sat up and knuckled a few steps from the nest—leaving Seek behind, blinking in irritable confusion at the chaos breaking out in the forest. Hope swelled in Chase's chest. The Silverback rose up on his hind legs and beat his chest, letting out a wild roar of anger.

"Rot-eaters!" he bellowed. "Find them! Kill th—"

But Ribsnapper had more planned than just cackling in the woods. Chase saw the commotion as she burst from the undergrowth, seized a nest of flattened leaves in her jaws, and shook it as hard as she could, sending leaves and moss and earth scattering everywhere. The stunned gorilla who'd been in the nest a moment before tried to grab for her. Her weak leg was much better now, and she evaded his grasp, but it was a close thing—his thick fingers closed where her neck had been a moment before.

"Get her!" the Silverback yelled, and more than half of the gorillas staggered up out of their nests and joined the hunt, barking and yelling at Ribsnapper. The Silverback didn't run, but stomped angrily across the clearing to observe.

"Now or never," Shadow breathed, and Chase nodded.

"Now!" she hissed.

Both of them leaped from their hiding place, Chase in front, Shadow somewhere behind her. She focused on nothing but getting to Seek, and made it in a short sprint, leaping over tree roots and springing up onto the raised rock where the Silverback's nest had been made.

Seek looked up at her and hissed. "No! I want to stay here!"

"Sorry, you don't get a say," Chase said. She snatched him up by the scruff and turned to jump down. She couldn't resist pausing, from this vantage point, to see what was happening. Gorillas were rushing to and fro, chaos reigning as they tried to find a pack of hyenas that wasn't there. Ribsnapper was nowhere to be seen. The Silverback was still looking away. . . .

But Shadow was trapped, facing off against a gorilla who'd turned at the wrong moment.

"Leopard! There's a leopard too!" the gorilla yelled, and the Silverback turned.

"Chase, run!" Shadow cried.

Chase leaped from the Silverback's nest and began to run, holding firmly on to Seek. She kept her eyes fixed on a gap between the trees. If she could just make it into the mist and vanish . . .

She made it through the gap, and then her vision blurred and pain throbbed around one of her eyes. She stumbled and fell, then realized what had happened.

It was Seek. He'd wriggled enough to rake a claw across her face. She tried to hold on to him, but he lashed out again, and she dropped him before he could do any more damage.

"Seek, *please*," she begged and reached out to pick him up again.

"Stop her!" howled the Silverback, and Chase looked up through her stinging eye and saw two blurs of black as the gorilla that had been cornering Shadow turned and started to run toward her. She turned her good eye to the threat and bared her fangs. She would stand between them and Seek, no matter what.

The gorilla reached out to grab her, but she bit it hard on the arm. It yelled and brought its other hand around in a stunning blow that blurred her vision in the other eye. More gorillas pounded across the forest floor, and in moments Chase was surrounded by blurs of black fur and furiously bared teeth. Fists came down on her legs and her chest, and for a moment, she remembered how they'd treated Prowl's body and thought she was about to suffer the same fate. But then she realized they were just leaning on her, pinning her down.

There was nothing she could do. The gorillas were too heavy, and there were too many to fight.

She went limp.

"I give up," she gasped.

The Silverback's face came into view, and he leaned down and spoke into her ear.

"Range has asked that we not kill you," he said. "You can thank him later."

He raised a fist. In desperation, Chase tried to lift her head, to beg Seek to run one last time.

But she couldn't see him. And she couldn't see Shadow, or Ribsnapper, or hear any sounds of fighting.

Could it be . . . ? she thought. *Did they get him away? Did we do it?*

The Silverback's fist came down, and she didn't think anything else.

CHAPTER NINETEEN

Bramble sat with his back against the big rock in the Great Father's clearing, watching Mud the baboon stare at stones.

Is this it? he thought as Mud bent over, cocked his head, squinted at the stones, and then scooped them all up into his palm, not for the first time since they'd met the Great Father. *Is this the end of our journey? We were too late. Did we walk too slowly? Was it because we got lost in the tunnels?*

Mud threw the stones again. They scattered in what looked like much the same way, and once again Mud sat and stared at them for a long time, examining them from every angle, poking one or two with a long finger.

"What is he doing?" Moonflower asked. She was pacing back and forth beside him, unable to settle. Bramble shook his head. He'd been watching Mud for ages, and he had no idea what the stones were or why the baboon never seemed satisfied with how they landed. "How can it be important right now?" Moonflower continued. "We need to work out what we're going to do about the sandtongues!"

"That's what he's trying to do," said a voice, and Moonflower jumped. Behind her, Spider, the strange troopless baboon, was approaching, with more fruits in his arms. He passed a guava to Moonflower and rolled a small mango over to Bramble, then sat down beside him and started to chew on one of his own. "Those stones are his way of communing with the Great Spirit," he said through a mouthful of mango. "They tell him the future."

Bramble looked up at Moonflower. "Like the Spirit Mouth?"

"Maybe," she said, frowning. "Do they work?"

"Depends who you ask," said Spider. "Mud would say yes. Me? I've never seen it, but I'm not a Starleaf. Different animals look for answers in different ways. Did you know that the banded mongoose colonies choose a new leader every new moon?"

Bramble shook his head morosely.

"They think the Great Spirit wants them to. I never figured out why, and I served as their leader for a month. The point is . . ." Spider hesitated. "What was my point? Oh—the stones help Mud, and Mud's going to help the rest of us, so we should let him get on with it."

Bramble wasn't sure that was the point, but he was too tired to challenge Spider on his nonsense.

Another three baboons emerged from behind the rock,

and Bramble recognized Cricket and Crab, two of the four baboons called Highleaves who had been set to guard the Great Father. The other baboon was one he hadn't seen before.

"Hello, Grub," said Spider, waving him over. "How is he?"

The baboon called Grub stared at Bramble and Moonflower, his eyes going wide.

"These are my gorilla friends," Spider said. "Bramble and Moonflower, this is Grub Goodleaf. He looks after his troop when they're sick."

Grub sighed and walked over to Spider, his feet dragging in the grass. "I've done all I can for Thorn," he said. "But he won't eat or drink. You have to make him drink something, Spider. Or get Mud to. Otherwise, the snake venom won't kill him, hunger and thirst will."

"This is nothing like what happened to Burbark," said Moonflower. "I don't understand it."

Grub looked at her curiously. "You've seen a snakebite like this before?"

"Our father was bitten," Bramble said. "And he started acting strangely too, but it wasn't like this. He seemed fine, at first, but then he . . ." He trailed off, suddenly uncertain how to even describe the horror that had overtaken the troop.

"He wanted everyone else to get bitten too," Moonflower said. "One by one, the madness took over the whole troop, until we were the only ones left. That's why we came here, to ask for the Great Father's help. But . . ."

Grub Goodleaf sighed and scratched his chest thoughtfully. "If it really is the same thing, then perhaps the Great

Spirit is helping Thorn fight the poison. But I think that's a question for Mud," he added. "He's the one who deals with spirits. I have to get back to the troop. I'll be back to check on Thorn again tomorrow, Spider. Cricket, you can send that young gazelle to fetch me if anything else happens."

He left, with Crab Highleaf walking alongside him.

Bramble stood up. Perhaps they had arrived too late to save Thorn, but if there was anything to be done to stop the evil from the mountain, he had to find a way to do it.

He headed over to where Mud was still sitting, staring at his stones with his chin resting in his hands. Moonflower and Spider followed after him.

"Mud?" he said. "I don't mean to interrupt. . . ."

Mud's head snapped up, as if he'd been startled. "Yes?"

"Can I ask, what do the stones say? Moonflower's our Mistback—I think that's a bit like a Starleaf," he added. "Maybe there's something she can do to help."

He glanced back at Moonflower, who nodded but didn't look at all certain.

Mud gave them both a long look, and Bramble couldn't help but feel they were both being assessed.

"I've asked the Spirit several times," he said at last. "And the answer is always the same. *One will come to save the Great Spirit.*"

"Oooh," said Spider. All three of the others looked at him. "Did it say Great Spirit, or Great Father?"

Mud squinted through his one good eye at Spider. "Spirit. I checked. Several times."

"Well then. Poor old Thorn," said Spider. "We need to

make plans, don't we, Mud? We can't have Bravelands go without a Great Father again. We need to find his successor before . . . Well, remember what happened with Titan?"

"I remember very well," Mud snapped. "But Thorn's not dead yet, and I won't have you talking like he is!"

"I didn't say that," said Spider, sounding hurt. "They're *your* stones, Mud. Make them say something else if you don't like it."

Bramble backed away, as the two elderly baboons began to bicker. This seemed like it had become personal.

"I'm going for a walk," he muttered to Moonflower. "I need to think."

"Bring some thoughts back for me, will you?" Moonflower said, with a faint smile that didn't quite hide how tired and lost she must be feeling.

"I'll try." Bramble knuckled slowly across the clearing and past the trees. He didn't know where he was going. He didn't want to go far. He just needed to be alone for a moment. The forest was hardly like their territory on the mountain at all, but it was still strangely comforting to swing himself up into a tall tree and climb and climb until he was on the last of the branches that would hold his weight.

Surrounded by gently wavering leaves, Bramble sat in the crook of a branch and picked at the bark, trying to think.

One will come . . .

Mud and Spider had immediately started arguing about the second part of Mud's message, but what if the first part was more important? Bramble wondered for a moment if it could be him or Moonflower—surely it was more likely to be Moonflower, since she had the connection to the Spirit that he didn't—but he thought it couldn't be either of them, since they'd arrived together. It didn't say, *One will come to save the Great Spirit and also her brother will be there.*

So who, or what, could it be? If he could figure that out, then perhaps he could fetch them, or do *something* to help.

Back on the mountain, he'd been so content. All he'd ever really wanted to do was follow Cassava around, prank Groundnut, and one day grow up to be a good Blackback. He hadn't even wanted to be Silverback. That was Cassava's destiny, not his.

Now all he wanted was a job to do. The mystery of the snakebites, the journey from the mountain—he'd gotten used to having a *mission*, and now that nobody knew what to do without the Great Father's guidance, it was like being back in that endless fog, wandering, hoping against hope that something would appear to help him through.

He couldn't even settle to napping or sitting and thinking in his tree for very long. He couldn't bear the idea that Thorn or Moonflower might need him and he wouldn't be around. So he climbed down and began to head back, taking the long way around through the trees.

As he approached the clearing, he saw one of the Highleaves—he thought it was the one called Acanthus—sitting down with his back against a tree, apparently napping. Was he asleep on the job? Bramble knew that there would be trouble if Mud caught him, so he knuckled over and reached out a hand to shake his shoulder.

But when he nudged Acanthus, the baboon slid over and fell into a stiff heap in the leaves, trailing blood from a deep bite wound in the side of his neck.

Bramble reeled back, his heart hammering. What had done this? He spun around, afraid that he'd see a lion creeping up to leap on him too—but there was nothing, and he scented nothing either, except mud and blood. . . .

But the blood scent led away from the body, and now that he was looking, there was a trail of broken undergrowth and crushed leaves through the forest. Whatever had killed Acanthus, it was on the move, and it was going . . .

Toward the Great Father's nest.

Bramble broke into a run, shouldering through a bush that scratched at him, stumbling and leaping over tree trunks. He saw the thick, flowering bushes that sheltered the Great Father, and then he saw the end of a thick tail vanishing as something with pale, furless skin slunk underneath the thick wooden stems.

Bramble punched both hands through the bushes and tugged their branches back with all his strength, breaking stems and scattering leaves as he pushed through.

The thing in Thorn's nest was massive, pale, and scaly, with thick arms and legs and a tail that lashed as it realized Bramble was right behind it. Thorn himself was slumped in the corner of the nest, his eyes wide and staring. The lizard creature turned its head and opened its mouth to taste the air, and Bramble recognized those milky eyes and strange flicking tongue.

It was the lizard that had attacked him at the gully.

Frightened and angry, Bramble let out a bellow and grabbed the creature by the tail, dragging it backward. It dug its claws into the ground, snapping and hissing at Thorn. Then suddenly it let go, turning on Bramble, and he tumbled onto his back. The lizard swarmed up and over him, and he tried to grip its head to stop it from biting, while its awful sharp claws pierced the skin on his side.

He heard Moonflower yelling his name, and Mud and Spider calling for Thorn, as he wrestled with the lizard, trying to ignore the pain. He rolled over, slamming the creature onto its back, but the thing was wriggling and writhing in his grasp. He was vaguely aware of scuffling and hooting as the baboons ran into the nest, but the lizard writhed again and managed to get right side up. It lunged, attempting to get out from underneath him, and he let out a furious yell and scooped it up in both arms, squeezing hard. It hissed and scratched and thumped him with its tail, but he pulled back, lifting its legs from the ground, and it couldn't get away.

He could see the other baboons now. Some were carrying Thorn from the nest. Cricket and Egg Highleaf were watching him, awe and terror on their faces.

"Help me!" Bramble grunted, but the baboons seemed too frightened. Moonflower ran toward him and tried to grab the lizard's tail, but with a last desperate spasm it clawed at the air, keeping her away.

Then, a moment later, the lizard stopped moving. Bramble looked down at its face and saw those horrible milky eyes half close, its tongue lolling limply from its jaws.

He dropped the creature and backed away, his hands shaking.

Whoops of triumph went up from baboons.

"Good work, Bramble!" Cricket hooted.

Bramble didn't feel good. He sat back heavily and stared at the lizard.

"Are you all right?" Moonflower said, putting her arms around him.

"Bruises," Bramble said faintly. He looked down at his side and saw red blood running through his fur. "And it clawed me, right here."

"We'll take care of it," Moonflower assured him. "You saved the Great Father!"

Bramble looked up. "Is Thorn . . ."

"He's a bit shocked, I think," Moonflower said. "But he's not hurt."

"You did well, Bramble," said Mud. Bramble looked over and saw the elderly Starleaf staring at him, as if reassessing him. His one good eye glinted.

The baboons were still hooting in triumph. Now they were trying to drag the body of the lizard away, though it was almost too heavy for them. Crab came up to Bramble and gave him a hearty pat on the back before running to help.

Bramble just stared at the eyes of the lizard as they pulled it through the leaves by the tail. They'd been blind, but there had been life. It had been breathing, and then it . . . stopped.

I killed another living thing, he thought. *I just killed it.*

He couldn't share the baboons' joy. He dropped his face into his hands so he couldn't see his victim anymore.

"Blood pools on the plains," he whispered to himself.

CHAPTER TWENTY

Prance woke up, stiff and sore, as if she'd been running all night—but she was back on the dewy grass, with Shortsight and the other bait creatures beside her. The sun was rising, throwing sharp spears of light into her eyes, and she got to her hooves and stretched, staring into the far, bright distance.

Had it been real? Truly, she wasn't certain. She thought it was, but running across the plains as her own shadow . . . It wasn't just that it sounded unlikely; it was more than that. She had some evidence that she had done *something* odd back in the Great Father's clearing, but what if her sleeping mind had taken that and run off with it into a vivid dream?

What if Moth and Gallant weren't even out there looking for her, let alone heading this way?

The lions around her were stirring, and Menace stretched and yawned hugely just as Prance saw something on the horizon. Running toward her, out of the dawn . . . It was a lion, with a long mane, crossing the plains with long strides. . . .

But it wasn't Gallant. Prance finally saw his face as he came closer, and it was one of Menacepride—the elderly male called Civil. He trotted up to the rest of the pride and sat down to scratch behind his ear with a back foot, dislodging a thin layer of dust from his thinning mane.

"Found some promising prey," he said as he scratched. "A herd of grasstongues, not far from here. They went into the mpaga forest."

"An excellent place for an ambush," said Menace with a cruel smile. "You, herd animals. Get up. You have work to do."

Prance shuddered. She knew the forest Civil meant. The trees there grew tall and spindly, and every one was draped in mpaga vines. Clusters of pale yellow flowers grew on the vines, disguising the fact that the vines themselves were thick and thorny, and would catch and tangle a herd animal who tried to storm through them in a panic.

"You newcomers," Menace said, turning on Prance and peering up at Shortsight. "You should know, if you don't play your parts, I will eat you. No excuses, no second chances. Got it?"

Shortsight hung his head miserably and whispered, "Yes."

Menace stared right into Prance's eyes until she also nodded.

They set off, a bizarre sight as they trudged across the plains—a gazelle, a giraffe, a zebra, and a tiny dik-dik all walking in sullen silence, flanked on all sides by mangy, scarred lions. Prance kept watch on the horizon, hoping against hope that she would see Gallant and Moth, or Sky and the elephants, or any other creature who could get word back to the Great Father about where she was. But the only creatures she saw were a colony of meerkats, who vanished into their burrows at the first scent of the approaching lions.

They came to the edge of the mpaga forest, and Menace called a halt, sniffing at the trees, her tail swishing. Prance wondered whether she was looking at the thick vines that wound around the trunk of the closest tree and thinking that they could catch just as painfully on a lion's fur as a gazelle's hide.

"You four, go in there and lure the herd out to us," she said. "And no tricks."

"No, Menace," said Flick, with an obsequious bow that made Prance feel sick. She trotted into the forest, and Prance, Shortsight, and Gloomfriend had no choice but to follow.

Despite the winding, thorny vines that curled up into huge bushes around many of the tree trunks, Prance remembered this forest as a cool, pleasant place. The morning sun cast dappled shadows through the leaves, and without the lions watching them, she could almost imagine there was nothing wrong.

We can just run, can't we? she thought. But Menace was smarter than that. She must have lions watching the edge of the forest, waiting for any herd animal who tried to make a break for it.

And there was Flick. The dik-dik would be sure to run straight back and tell Menace if the rest of them tried to escape.

The forest wasn't large, and it didn't take long before Prance heard the sound of muffled voices. The shapes of brown and tan bodies started to appear in the gaps between the trees, their heads bent to graze on the grass and leaves.

Shock ran through Prance, like a lightning bolt through a dark sky.

It was Runningherd. They were all present—Bolt, Fleet, Scamper, old Thunder, and baby Leap . . . and Skip. Prance's best friend was there, her head rising as she sensed the newcomers approaching.

Prance saw the surprise and joy in Skip's eyes when she realized who was walking toward her, and she felt her insides squirm, tying themselves in anxious knots.

"Prance!" Skip cried. More of the gazelles looked up or walked carefully around the trees to get a better look. Many of them seemed delighted to see her, and even those who seemed wary or tossed their heads with nervousness didn't run from her.

The Us says I'm not a threat, Prance thought, and her heart broke at the horrible, horrible irony of it.

"What are you doing here?" Skip bounced up to Prance and pressed her nose to Prance's. "Who are your friends?"

"I . . . I . . ." Prance was too overcome to speak.

"We've come to warn you!" Flick said. Prance and Skip both stared down at her—Skip looking nervously interested, Prance feeling absolutely dismayed. "There are lions coming! But it's okay. If you come with us, we'll get out of the forest before they find us!"

Skip gasped. "Oh! Thank you for warning us! I'll get the others. . . ."

"No!" Prance yelled.

Her voice seemed to echo in the forest. Birds took off from the branches of a nearby tree, and the Runningherd gazelles fell silent, watching her with ears pricked. Prance could see the Us working behind their eyes.

Good! It's not safe here! I'm a danger to you all now. . . .

"Prance," said Gloomfriend, his voice shaking, "what are you doing?"

"I won't allow it," Prance said, her voice trembling too. "Flick is lying. This is a trap. The lions caught us yesterday, they made us come in here to lure you out." She looked deep into Skip's eyes, praying that the Us would tell her that Prance was telling the truth, that the danger was real. "It's a trap, but you still have time to get away. You have to run, now!"

A ripple of movement started behind Skip. Prance could sense the panic as it swelled up among the gazelles, and then they were turning to run. She could see the Us at work, driving every gazelle in the same direction.

Every gazelle except for Skip.

"You're in big trouble now," muttered Flick, backing away from Prance. Gloomfriend and Shortsight looked at each other, and then they joined Flick. Prance didn't blame them.

"Go!" she said to Skip, nudging her with her horns. "Listen to the Us and *run!*"

Skip shook her head. "No, not without you! We've got time, I still have a—"

But she looked down, and her words cut off. Prance followed her gaze and let out a shaky breath of horror.

Skip's shadow was gone.

"No," Prance said. "Please, you have to run, you have to try. . . ."

"But—where's the Us? Where did it go? What do I—" Skip began, but then a tawny blur streaked across Prance's vision, so close she could smell the stink of lion, and then Skip was on the ground, and Menace's fangs were buried in her neck.

Prance screamed and stumbled backward.

Menace looked up, Skip's blood dripping from her muzzle. Skip twitched once under her paws and lay still, the same look of horror on her face that she'd had when she realized the Us was gone.

"Menacepride," said Menace, and Prance threw a look over her shoulder to see the rest of the lions stalking up behind her. "We will eat well today. Kill this disloyal, herdless thing."

Prance let out a high-pitched yell and broke into a sprint, digging her hooves into the soft forest floor, galloping right at Menace. Menace's surprise bought her the split second's grace she needed—at the last minute she dodged to the side, avoiding the lioness's claws, ducked underneath a trailing mpaga vine, and bolted into the forest.

She couldn't think, couldn't stop. She heard the lions pounding after her.

How many?

Doesn't matter—it takes only one to catch and kill me. RUN.

She dodged and weaved around the trees, kicking up leaves

as she pronked to avoid a spreading mpaga bush.

What about Shortsight?

He made the right choice. He's safe for now. Nothing you can do. KEEP RUNNING.

A lion let out a roar of pain and irritation behind her.

Just. Keep. Running.

Zigzagging, smacking her side into tree trunks, using her horns to toss branches out of the way, catching her own skin on the thorns as she pushed through a gap only just big enough to take her, she ran as if the Us were with her, driving her on, leaving no time to think or question, only to find the way and then take it.

But the lions were clever. To her left she heard a growl, and she realized one of them had circled around, blocking the way she wanted to go. She took a hard right turn and almost ran face-first into an mpaga bush. She had to stop to find a way to go, and all the time the lions were on her tail.

All too soon, the panic couldn't seem to drive her on anymore, and even the thought of Skip under Menace's claws didn't overcome the pain in her legs, or the way her heart felt like it was about to climb up out of her throat. She stumbled on as long as she could, taking every unexpected turn, dodging and weaving, but she knew she was slowing down.

"Got her!" cried a lion voice. It was the young one, Terror. Prance jumped out of the way to avoid him as he made a great leap for her, and his claws missed raking across her flank, but she stumbled right into a tree trunk and came to an undignified, exhausted halt.

The lions slunk into view all around her. There was no sign of Menace. Prance tried not to think about what she was doing right now.

"Good, Terror," said Civil. "Your mother will be proud of you. Go on—take the kill for yourself."

Suddenly, Terror looked nervous. He paused, staring at Prance as if trying to steel himself for this.

He's just a cub, she thought. *He's never taken down prey like me before.*

She knew she should have taken the opportunity to flee again, but she was just too tired. Her legs could hardly lift her back to her hooves.

"Hurry up," said one of the other lionesses. "Before it gets away."

"I'll do it," sighed another lion. "If you're too soft, *Terror*." He stalked forward, and Prance lowered her horns, prepared to try to spear him on them, even if it might mean they both died. . . .

Then the older lion looked up, and his jaw went slack with surprise, a moment before a mighty roar sounded from behind Prance's shoulder, and a large, healthy-looking lion bounded through the trees and stood in front of her.

"You leave her alone!" yelled the baboon who rode on his back. She leaped off and climbed up onto Prance instead, hugging her around the neck.

"Gallant!" Prance gasped. "Moth, you found me!" She felt faint with relief. Moth stroked the back of her head with a reassuring hand.

"Leave," said Gallant. "Now."

"That's *our* prey," said Civil. "You've no right . . ."

"*Now!*" Gallant roared, then raised one huge paw and swiped it down across the old lion's face. Civil backed up, bleeding from where one of Gallant's claws had caught the side of his nose.

"Menace will kill you one day, Blood of Fearless," Civil snarled. "And I hope to be there to watch."

"Menace can't even catch her own prey without using bait to lure it in," Gallant snarled back. "Tell her I'll be waiting for her."

The lions started to move away, skulking backward until they felt safe enough to turn their backs on Gallant and begin to run.

The last one to leave was Terror. Gallant turned on him, ready to roar again, and then froze. He stared at the cub, and the cub stared at him, treading the leaves nervously under his front paws.

"*Valorcub* . . . ?" Gallant whispered.

"What?" the cub hissed back. "My name is Terror. . . ." But he was staring at Gallant as if he knew him, sniffing him as if his scent was familiar.

They were almost the same height, though Terror was much skinnier. The hints of a mane that were coming through on the back of Terror's neck were the same color as Gallant's. Prance felt Moth's hands tighten on her and knew she must be coming to the same realization that Prance was.

Terror is Gallant's lost cub!

"Terror . . ." Gallant frowned. "How old are you? When did you join this pride?"

Terror was shaking his head and trying to growl, but it came out squeaky and afraid. "I was born in it!" he said.

"No, you weren't. You're not Terror. You're Valorcub. You're *my cub!*" Gallant started forward, his voice cracking. But Terror flinched and backed away.

"You're not my father," he muttered. "I have no father. Menace is my mother, she's the only family I have."

Gallant stopped in his tracks. "*Menace?*" he growled.

Terror turned and ran. Gallant took a few steps, looking like he might follow.

"Gallant," Moth called. "Prance needs you."

"I'm all right," Prance said, but her voice came out fainter than she'd expected. She tried to stand and walk, but her legs shook and she fell to her knees, Moth sliding from her back just in time to steady her on the way down.

Gallant turned back and saw her, then looked back at the forest where Terror had slipped away. He squeezed his eyes shut and let out a long, pained sigh.

"All right," he said. "We should get you out of here."

He lowered his head and gently nudged Prance back to her hooves.

"You can lean on me," he said.

Prance had half expected him to be angry with her. She'd run away when he'd told her to stay put, and now because of her he'd had to let his cub go. . . .

To think your cub was lost, to find him again, and then be torn away to look after someone else . . . She couldn't imagine the pain he must be in. But if Gallant was angry, he didn't show it. Prance managed to walk, leaning against the lion's soft fur, and before too long she found her own hooves again and stumbled along under her own power until they came to the edge of the mpaga forest.

She stopped and turned back. Somewhere in that mess of vines and tree branches, Skip lay dead, and Great Spirit knew what had happened to Shortsight.

And it was all her fault.

"Thank you for coming," she murmured, and Moth laid a warm, reassuring paw on her side. Prance tried to smile at her, but she couldn't. Right now, she wasn't sure she'd ever feel anything but numb horror again.

The curse of the shadowless does follow me, she thought. *I tried to help the giraffes, and I got their foal taken. The Us thought I wasn't a threat, right when I was about to get Skip killed.*

Why am I alive? What is it the Great Spirit wants from me?

CHAPTER TWENTY-ONE

Chase stumbled dizzily as a gorilla shoved her. Her head was throbbing from the Silverback's punch. One of them had her tail gripped in its fist, and another had her by the scruff. She wasn't fighting—there was no point. In the dark, the gorillas surrounding her were like a solid wall of black fur, grasping hands, and glinting eyes. She was bleeding; she could taste blood in her mouth and feel it running down her front leg and over her paw. Whenever she moved, she felt a sharp stabbing in her side. Was one of her ribs broken?

"Kill her, Burbark," said one of the Blackbacks.

The Silverback peered down at Chase, and she managed to raise her head and look him in the eye. He was a terrifying sight from so close up, a massive figure against the stars, baring his long yellow fangs in a snarl.

If you're going to do it, then do it, she thought. *You can stomp my body into the ground just like you did my mother, I don't care, as long as Seek's made it out.* . . .

Burbark Silverback raised his fist once more as his troop hooted and called for Chase's death. Chase refused to close her eyes, fixing her gaze on Burbark. She wouldn't look away. He would have to make her.

"Stop!"

A low growl reverberated between the trees. Burbark lowered his fist just a little and slowly turned, opening up a line of sight from Chase to Range as he climbed down from the trees and stalked toward them.

"Let her go," Range said. His tail swished, and he bared his teeth at the gorilla that held Chase's scruff.

"And who are you to give my troop orders?" Burbark snapped.

Chase's vision was swimming, but she thought she saw Range's expression change, from angry to coolly thoughtful, as he sat back on his haunches and licked one paw.

"My apologies, Silverback," he said smoothly. "I didn't mean to overstep. But with the loss of the cub, this adult leopard is surely even more valuable to our cause? She will be more useful in the coming battles than Seek could be. Let Grandmother show her that the only way to protect the cub is to fight with us, and she'll walk over hot steam to do it—you've seen that dedication for yourself," he added.

"I'll never be your ally," Chase spat.

"Burbark, it's too dangerous," said one of the Goldbacks. "We could have raised the cub as one of us, but not this stubborn female. Kill her and be done with it."

Burbark scratched his chest, deep in thought. All the gorillas turned their heads to watch him patiently waiting for his verdict.

Range, though, kept his eyes fixed on Chase.

"Consider your choices carefully," he muttered. "If you antagonize us, I can't help you. But if you surrender now and take Grandmother's blessing, then you won't just live. You'll have territory. You'll have *family*. One day, perhaps cubs of your own. You can have a future, or you can die, here and now."

Chase gritted her teeth and took the deepest breath she could manage, still grappled by the gorillas.

"You're right," she grunted. "I'm sorry."

Burbark turned to stare at her, and Chase swallowed hard.

"Why should we believe you?" he rumbled.

"I—I was so angry," she said, as meekly as she could. "I missed my cub so much. But . . . Range is right, I can't fight you. I'll do whatever you want. I just want to live and see my cub again."

She could hear the gorillas muttering to one another. She could tell that not all of them believed her. But Burbark was the only one she needed. She let in the fear that she'd been fighting, trembling as he looked up at him.

"There's no harm in testing her resolve," Range said. "Either the blessing will take hold, or she'll be too weak and won't make it anyway."

"Please," Chase begged. "I'll take any test. I will pledge myself to you, if that's what you want."

"Not to us," said Range. "To Grandmother."

Burbark reached out, and something started to move up his arm, curling its way round and round until its head peeked over his shoulder. A snake, of course. She should have been expecting it, but she still flinched, looking into its beady black eyes, knowing that it had just been *there*, watching, waiting. Burbark handled it gently, respectfully, letting it wind its way down his other arm toward her. It settled on his wrist, its black tongue flicking out, just a few claw-lengths from Chase's nose. Instinctively she tried to pull back, but the gorilla holding her just tightened his grip, almost choking her.

"Do not fear," said Burbark, his voice strangely distant, almost gentle. "The pain is brief, but Her gift is eternal. Prove your fealty. Accept the bite."

Chase dragged in another deep breath, doing her best to suppress her shudder, as Burbark brought the snake lower and lower, letting it sniff around her throat.

Hold on, she thought. *Just hold on. They bit me before, and the rot-meat protected me. I've eaten more since then. Just remember why we're doing this. . . .*

Stiffly, she raised one paw and held it out in front of her. She shut her eyes. She didn't want to see the moment it bit her. . . .

"Good," said Range. "That's good, Chase. It'll be over soon."

Something stabbed into Chase's back leg. Shock made her open her eyes and look around.

Burbark wasn't the only gorilla holding a snake. *All* of them were. The gorillas swayed along with their hissing, writhing brethren, and Chase let out a terrified whine as the venom from the first to strike coursed up her leg, and the gorillas brought their snakes closer. Burbark's moved like lightning and bit Chase in the cheek. She yowled and stumbled, vaguely aware of the gorillas' grip loosening on her scruff and her tail, before she could be aware of nothing but the shuddering pain and horror as snake after snake lashed out and sank its fangs into her foreleg, her flank, her tail, the back of her head.

She screamed as the burning venom throbbed in her blood, and she fell to the ground. She wasn't sure now if she was still being bitten, or if she was just twitching so hard it felt like being struck again and again. Blood streamed into her eye, she couldn't think . . .

"It'll be all right," whispered a voice close to her ear. Range. "You'll be fine. I'll take care of you."

At last, to Chase's relief, she fell into blackness, and it swallowed her whole.

"I can't do it." Chase born of Prowl tried to dig her claws into the tree branch, *but even that small movement made her wobble and almost lose her balance. She dropped to her belly and squeezed her eyes closed. "I can't!"*

"Yes, you can." Prowl's voice was gentle but firm, and Chase hated it. She squeezed her eyes even more tightly shut and pressed her forehead to the branch.

"I can not! I'll fall and hit my head and die, and then you'll be sorry."

Ahead of her she heard an amused mew from her mother, which was even more annoying. But she didn't say anything else. Eventually, Chase opened one eye, then the other, and looked down over the edge of the branch. The ground was a long way away.

Prowl was sitting in the next tree, watching her. Chase didn't want to move, but it was getting tiring, clinging to the branch with all her strength. She looked away from her mother and started to get up, placing her large cub paws gingerly in front of her. The branch swayed, and Chase gasped and looked up at Prowl again. Prowl blinked calmly at her.

"You can trust your paws, Chase," said Prowl. "And your tail. They won't let you down if you listen to them."

Chase fixed her eyes on the end of the branch. All she had to do was get as far as the other, thicker branch that crossed it, and then she'd be in the next tree, beside her mother.

"Can't you help me?" she asked in a small voice. "Just this once?"

"That's not the way of leopards," Prowl reminded her. "You can't rely on another leopard to be there all the time; you must rely on yourself. Trust only yourself."

Trust only myself. . . . Chase took a deep breath and put one paw forward on the branch. She tried to listen to what her tail was telling her—mostly it was telling her it was stiff and scared and it wanted to get down. But slowly, paw by paw, using her twitching tail for balance, she made it to the next branch. It dipped beneath her weight as she put her paws up on it, and she almost froze, but instead she bunched her muscles and leaped, or at least hopped, onto the new branch.

"I did it!" she purred and ran the rest of the way to Prowl's side.

Prowl licked the top of her head, purring back. "I'm so proud of you," she said.

Chase felt her mother's tail wrap around her, as it did at home in their den.

But instead of the thick, fluffy fur that kept her warm on cold nights, Prowl's tail felt hard and smooth, and it moved wrong. She felt muscles moving that shouldn't be there. She looked up at her mother and saw that her eyes were black beads, and her muzzle opened to reveal two wickedly sharp fangs, dripping with venom, and a black forked tongue that whipped out and flicked across Chase's nose. Chase recoiled.

"Mother?" she yowled.

"Your mother is dead," the creature hissed. "Trust only me. Trust only Grandmother."

Chase jerked awake and then fell back, her sides heaving. Her whole body ached, a feeling like the very worst stomachache she'd ever had, but everywhere, from the tips of her ears to the end of her tail. One moment she felt as if she was swaddled in suffocating warmth, the next she thought it must be snowing on the mountain as shivers and trembling seized her.

"Are you awake?" said Range. She peered up at him.

"Ugh," she said.

Range leaned over and licked the top of her head. Chase shuddered.

"How are you doing?" he asked. He sounded pleased. "I told them you were strong. I knew you'd live through this."

Was the ache subsiding, or was she just getting used to it? Either way, Chase was surprised to find the strength returning to her limbs, at least enough that she could roll over and lie on her belly, instead of flat out on her side. She squinted at Range, and then around at the forest.

Where were they? It wasn't the same place as the gorilla

nests. She must have been unconscious for a long time, because strong sunshine filtered down through the tree branches . . . and through a twisting mass of snakes.

Chase startled, and then stared. The trees were full of snakes, but not just living ones—their long bodies wove between what looked like branches full of ghosts. The discarded skins of snakes hung limply overhead, silvery and horrible.

Don't worry, said a voice, and Chase startled again and looked behind her. *Trust Grandmother. One day you will all shed your skins and be reborn as your true selves.*

The tone of the voice was deep and soothing, slightly sibilant, but very calm.

It was only the words that made Chase's heart race.

Range was watching her, his eyes wide with excitement. "You can hear her, can't you?"

"What *is* it?" Chase said.

"Chase, it's *Grandmother*," Range said. His eyes shone and he moved up to her side and licked her head again. "I'm so happy for you. She's chosen you to be one of us. It means you're worthy! I always knew you were. . . ."

The Age of Sandtongue comes, the voice went on. Chase listened in horrified fascination, ignoring Range's enthusiasm. It didn't seem like Grandmother could hear her thoughts in return—the deep, soothing voice just kept repeating its strange mantras. Was this what Range and Burbark and all the gorillas were hearing all the time? *Rise, my children, and greet the new day. Bravelands waits for you. The cleansing must begin. The Age of*

Sandtongue will be an age of true freedom. Each one of you will be free from the tyranny of the Great Spirit. . . .

Chase could almost feel herself being lulled by the voice. It would be so easy to simply lie here and listen, even if she didn't believe it. And how long would it take for listening to become believing?

She took a deep breath and concentrated on her *own* thoughts, the ones she knew came from inside, not somewhere else.

I am Chase, daughter of Prowl, she thought. *I am a leopard. I am still free.*

Her own voice could block out the voice of Grandmother, at least for a little while. Chase looked up at Range and forced herself to smile.

I am Chase, daughter of Prowl, she thought. *And I trust only myself.*

CHAPTER TWENTY-TWO

What new horrible thing is happening now? Bramble wondered as the vultures circled above the corpses of the rock monitor lizard and Acanthus Highleaf.

One of them finally landed, and then another. They danced around the bodies for a moment, and then one leaned down and pecked at the lizard's skin until it could tear off a piece.

Is there anything on the plains that doesn't somehow come down to blood? Bramble thought.

"The vultures taste the death," Mud told him, as if that was a perfectly natural thing to say. "They can taste whether the death was a good one or not. If it was, then they all eat. If not . . ." He broke off as the vulture who had tasted the lizard's flesh gave a shrill cry.

The vulture who had hopped over to peck at Acanthus startled and shrieked back at its companion. Both of them opened their large wings and flapped and shrieked, the feathers on the backs of their necks puffing up, as if in fear or anger. And then they both leaped into the sky, without even tasting the corpse of Acanthus. The one who had tasted the lizard led the way, still screaming out a hoarse cry, and the others followed suit. Bramble watched with a shudder as their flock split and reformed, changing from the circling cloud to a curious, snaking path through the sky.

"What does *that* mean?" he said.

Mud didn't answer for a moment, and Bramble looked down at him. He was dismayed to see a look of confusion and worry pass over the old baboon's face. Then Mud shook himself.

"Perhaps nothing," he said.

Perhaps? Bramble cast a horrified glance at Moonflower. *Perhaps it means it was a "bad death"—perhaps it means I've done something even worse than I thought!*

"You did the right thing," Moonflower said as the Highleaves moved in to drag the rock monitor out of the clearing once more. "You saved the Great Father. They must be able to see that."

But did I? Bramble glanced back at the Great Father's nest. Thorn was asleep now, or semiconscious—it was hard to tell which.

That hadn't been the case immediately after the lizard attack. At first, the Great Father had refused to lie down or even sit down. He had leaned on his stick, staring at nothing, and then he'd started dragging the stick through the mud and leaves, adding curves to the strange swirling pattern he had been drawing since the snake bit him. Bramble had watched the Highleaves and Mud and Spider all try to get Thorn to lie down, worry in their faces as he staggered, his breath coming heavy and labored as he sketched in the dirt. But Thorn wouldn't let them escort him back to his nest, until suddenly the energy seemed to leave him and he slumped into a stupor.

"Where did this thing come from, anyway?" Crab grunted as the Highleaves hefted the big lizard against a tree stump. "I've never seen anything like this before!"

"Poor Acanthus," said Egg. "He must have had no idea what hit him."

"I—I think I know where it came from," Bramble said. All the baboons turned to look at him, and he took a deep breath. "I think we saw it on our way here from the mountain. It attacked me when we were still a long way from here. I think it's followed us ever since."

The Highleaves gaped at him.

"I think it's possible it followed us all the way here from the mountain," Moonflower muttered. "After all, that was the Spirit's message. *Evil spreads from the mountain, unless wisdom stands in its path. . . .*"

Bramble shuddered and gave Moonflower a horrified look.

What if we fulfilled the prophecy by coming here? What if we brought the evil with us?

"Did you see it following you?" Mud asked.

"No," said Bramble. "But I'm sure it was the same one that attacked us."

"Bramble," said Spider, who had gone over to Acanthus's body and was sitting beside it. "Where did you find Acanthus? Can you show me?"

Bramble sighed and got to his feet. He wasn't sure why Spider wanted to know, but he led him through the trees anyway. It wasn't hard to find the spot where Acanthus had died—the tree, and the ground, were splattered with blood. He could smell it from the edge of the clearing. He stood well back and let Spider approach the tree and sniff at the disturbed leaves. Mud, Crab, and Moonflower had all followed them and now stood back, watching. Bramble wondered what the strange old baboon was looking for.

Spider turned on the spot, pointing first at the tree, then toward the Great Father's nest, spun and pointed in the opposite direction, and then started to walk.

"Ah," he said, pointing down at the leaves. Bramble took a few steps toward him, trying to see what he was looking at. "Careful! Keep those big feet that side of the tree, please," said Spider. "There's a trail. Look at these leaves."

Bramble stood as tall as he could and peered at the leaves. With a shock, he realized Spider was right—there was a trail, a clear path through the leaves, as if a large, heavy creature had dragged itself through the undergrowth toward the Great Father's nest.

"Follow me," Spider said and set off at a hopping run. Bramble followed after him, trying to make sure he didn't trample the trail.

They didn't have to go far. Spider stumbled to a clumsy halt and leaned on a boulder beside a large bush, getting his breath back. Bramble approached and looked for the trail, his frown deepening as he realized that he could trace it up to the bush, but then it just seemed to vanish, without coming out through the other side. If the lizard had run around the boulder or through the bush, it had left no trace.

Spider pointed to the bush.

"Would you mind?" he said.

Bramble felt his jaw go slack as he understood what Spider meant, and all at once, he knew exactly where the lizard had come from and how it had followed them here.

Spider stepped back as Bramble bent down and pushed the branches of the bush aside, snapping them off to reveal the deep, dark hole underneath.

"The tunnels," Bramble said. He looked around and saw Moonflower, Crab, and Mud all approaching, having followed at a cautious pace behind them. "It's the tunnels that Spider showed us before. That's how the lizard came all the way here from the gully. . . . They must run under all of Bravelands!"

"All the way to the mountains," Spider said. "I told you."

Moonflower stared at the hole and took a deep, apprehensive breath before she spoke. "Bramble, do you think these link to the tunnels under the Spirit Mouth?"

Bramble met her eyes and saw them glisten with fear, and with grief. It had been in the tunnels under the mountain that they'd lost Dayflower.

Bramble shuddered. "I think they might," he said.

"Should we go in there?" Crab asked. "I mean, the lizard's

gone now. There wouldn't be another one just lurking in there. Would there?"

There was a long silence as each of the baboons and gorillas stared at the dark hole in the ground and imagined what might be down there—at least, that was what Bramble was doing.

"This is what the Spirit Mouth sent us to warn you all about," Moonflower said. "It must be. *Evil will flow from the mountain*, just like the water in these tunnels."

"And I don't think that lizard is the end of it," Bramble said. "We need to make sure nothing else can come up through here."

"What do we do?" Crab asked, grasping his tail nervously.

"We need to collapse the tunnel," said Mud.

Spider made a doubtful noise. "If there's another lizard lurking in there, it will be able to dig its way out again if we just close this off."

Bramble swallowed.

"Someone needs to go deeper in," he said, a cold dread settling in his fur even as he said it. "Collapse it farther down."

He looked at the baboons. Crab was still passing his tail through his shaky paws, and Mud and Spider were leaning on their boulders and sticks. Not one of them was strong enough to actually do what needed to be done.

"I'll come with you," Moonflower said.

Bramble gave her a grateful smile, but then shook his head. "If I cause a collapse and then have to run for it, it'll be easier with one."

"Well," Moonflower said, "be careful. Don't go too far. Don't get lost."

Bramble felt a paw on his arm and looked down to see Mud standing there. He gave Bramble's arm a quick squeeze. "Thank you, Bramble. You will be all right," he said. "The Great Spirit will go with you."

I hope so, Bramble thought. He nodded at Mud, and then turned and let himself down into the darkness.

The first few gorilla-lengths weren't too claustrophobic. The entrance behind the boulder turned out to lead down a mud slope into a cave where the walls were mostly stone, and it was wide and tall enough for Bramble to stand up and stretch out his arms. But leading off the cave, through an arch of boulders, the tunnel was the same dark, cramped kind of space that Spider had led them into.

With a heavy sigh, he bent down and began to crawl.

The tunnel grew darker as he left the shaft of light from the entrance cave behind him. He could make out the floor in front of him, faint and fuzzy in the dim light, but little beyond the reach of his arm. His heart started to thump in his chest, and he paused. At least he could do that this time—he wasn't rushing to get to the other side of the river, and crucially, there was nobody there to see if he needed to steady himself.

His heart didn't stop pounding, but he began to get used to it as he pressed on into the darkness. The tunnel began to slope down, gently at first, and then much more sharply, until it evened out—or he thought it did. It was strangely hard to tell, with nothing but his sense of balance and the feeling of his knees and knuckles on the hard earth.

The air was starting to feel clammy now, and Bramble shuddered. It was so dark, he could imagine crawling straight into a crocodile, waiting with its eyes wide and its jaws ready to snap down on his head.

But it wasn't just the crocodiles this time.

When Spider had brought them down into the tunnels before, Bramble had been so preoccupied about whether Spider knew what he was doing, and then with the adrenaline of escaping the crocodiles, that it hadn't occurred to him that they had faced sandtongue creatures in dark spaces once before, very recently.

Something in the dark beneath the Spirit Mouth had taken Dayflower from them. Something enormous, which hissed as it dragged her down into the tunnels. Suddenly Bramble found himself imagining, not a crocodile, or even a monster, but *Dayflower*, crawling toward him in the dark with blank, dead eyes. . . .

Something made a sound up ahead. Bramble jumped, bumped his head, and in a panic lashed out with one fist. It passed harmlessly through the air and thumped into the ground, and a few tiny pieces of earth fell from the ceiling, with just the same sound that he'd heard the first time.

He could smell that the lizard had come this way, but other than its faint, dusty sandtongue scent, there didn't seem to be anything more down here to find, apart from trouble.

I should collapse this place and get out now, he told himself.

He took a few more steps into the darkness, sniffing the

air and feeling the walls and floor for a place where the mud would be soft enough to pull down.

His knuckles dragged across something strange. It was . . . soft. Silky. He yelped and reached a trembling hand out to touch it with his fingers.

It was too dark to see what he had, but he knew that feeling. His heart began to thump in his chest again as he pulled it toward him and found that it was huge and heavy. Perhaps he was wrong.

Oh, Great Spirit, please let me be wrong. . . .

He tried to pull it toward him, but it was too huge to gather and carry. He would have to drag it, and that meant not collapsing the tunnel after all. He hesitated for a moment, but the strange and terrible texture of the thing in his hands decided it for him.

He managed to turn around and, with the silky thing gripped tight in one hand, he hurried back toward the light, dragging it behind him. As he reached the cavern where the light flowed in from above and heard Moonflower's voice crying to the others that she could see him, he looked down at the thing he was carrying.

It was thin and translucent, delicate, slightly ripped in places from its journey up the tunnel, and unmistakably patterned with the imprints of what had once been scales.

He clambered out of the hole and pulled the thing up with him—or he started to. The others jumped and then gathered around to stare in horror as Bramble pulled and pulled, and the enormous snakeskin unfurled from the hole in the ground and pooled around his feet on the floor. After a moment's shock, Spider began hunting through the coils and found the head. He started to walk slowly backward, unspooling the skin. Crab and Moonflower joined him, holding portions of the snake in trembling, disbelieving paws.

The snakeskin was easily wide enough that Bramble could have climbed inside. In fact, Bramble noted with a dull horror on top of the creeping dread he'd been feeling since he touched the skin, it was about the same width as the tunnels. And by the time the end of the tail slithered out of the hole and into Bramble's hands, Spider had walked for four or five elephant-lengths—so far, he was almost standing in the Great Father's clearing.

"We should take this to Thorn," Mud whispered. He was staring at the snakeskin, but his clear eye was unfocused, as if he was actually looking at something beyond it that only he could see.

They carried the huge skin back to the clearing, a shudder crawling over Bramble's spine every step of the way. Egg and Cricket looked up as they stepped out of the trees, and their jaws dropped. Cricket covered her mouth as if she might be sick.

"I'll see if the Great Father's awake," Bramble said, excited for the excuse to drop his end of the skin. He hurried over to Thorn's nest, being careful not to scuff the long, sinuous lines Thorn had drawn on the ground. . . .

Then he stopped in his tracks. He looked down at the lines

and felt the same sick, sinking feeling he'd felt when he first picked up the snakeskin. He had less basis for it this time, but he felt just as certain, and the certainty was just as horrible.

"Spider," he said faintly. "Bring the head end over here?"

"You want to show it to Thorn?" Spider said, walking over with the giant, translucent snake's head held above his own, which made the ghostly thing look much more alive than it should have. "Are you sure? We don't want to give him a fright."

Bramble put his head into the nest and saw, without surprise, that Thorn was still sleeping fitfully, his breaths shallow and fast, and his eyes closed.

"I think . . . I think he's been expecting it," Bramble said.

He took the head of the snake from Spider and gingerly placed it down on the ground, where Thorn's stick had come to rest. Then slowly, methodically, he started to drag the snakeskin so that it lay along the lines that Thorn had drawn.

"Oh *no*," he heard Moonflower say, and a moment later she stepped up to help him, feeding the skin along gently so it didn't break, and nudging it into place so that every part of the line was covered. They worked together in near silence, while Mud and Spider and the Highleaves looked on, until they came to the tail end of the snake, and Bramble laid it down, without much ceremony, onto the very end of Thorn's drawing.

He looked up at Mud and bit his lip as he saw the old baboon's eyes turn wide and fearful.

The snake fit the line exactly. Stepping back, it looked very much like the Great Father was lying prone in the coils of the snake.

"Prance was right," Mud said faintly. Bramble looked at him with curiosity. Who was Prance? "And Spider, too. This . . . this . . . *beast*. It can travel to the plains at will, underground, and unseen. Evil is not on its way, Bramble. It is already here."

CHAPTER TWENTY-THREE

"Prance was right," Mud said. *Prance* stopped at the edge of the clearing, startled at hearing her own name the moment she came in view of the gathering.

She didn't immediately hear the rest of his sentence—she was distracted by what a strange gathering it was. The clearing was deserted, except for a group who seemed to be huddled around Thorn's nest. She couldn't see Thorn himself, but Mud was there, with three of the Highleaves and another baboon she didn't know, and alongside them, the largest monkeys Prance had ever seen. They were hulking and black, twice the size of the largest baboons, with black fur and flat, leathery gray faces. What *were* they? What was going on?

Gallant obviously felt just as startled, because he growled, low in his chest, and started across the clearing at a run.

"Mud?" he snarled. "What's going on? Where's the Great Father?"

"Gallant!" Mud said. He held up a placating hand, and Gallant slowed to a walk. Prance followed him, Moth still sitting on her back. She was watching the faces of the huge monkeys and saw that both of them had almost fallen over with fear as they'd seen the lion running toward them.

"It's all right . . . ," Mud said, and then sighed. He paused long enough for Prance to think he might be reconsidering how true that was. "These are friends," he said, laying a hand on the male's arm.

One of the other baboons stepped forward, and Prance felt Moth slide from her back.

"Father," she said. "What are you doing here?"

"Lovely to see you too, Moth," said the baboon with a smile. "I brought these gorillas to see the Great Father. Their names are Bramble and Moonflower. They came all the way here with a message from the mountain. Bramble, Moonflower, this is Gallant, my daughter Moth, and the gazelle is Prance. You can trust Gallant," he said, obviously realizing that they were both still staring at the lion with abject terror in their faces. "He won't hurt you."

"I'm glad they found you," said Mud, approaching Prance. He looked up into her face. She wondered if he might tell her he was wrong about his vision, but his gaze was curious and cool, not in the least bit soft or sorry. "We know now that you were right about the sandtongues," he admitted. "But I'm afraid it's too late. There was another attack.

Bramble here saved Thorn's life."

Gallant's ears flicked back in alarm, and he looked away. But the gorilla, Bramble, didn't exactly seem proud of himself either. He gave a heavy sigh and scratched his chest.

"Prance has more news of the sandtongues too," Gallant said.

Prance nodded. "I left because I wanted to talk to the giraffes," she said. "I found their leader, Broadsight—he had been bitten, and it drove him mad. First he wanted to take his herd to the mountain, then he tried to make them go to war against the hyenas. The hyenas killed him."

"The sandtongue sickness," muttered the female gorilla, Moonflower. She stepped forward, putting a hand on Bramble's shoulder. "Our father Burbark is the Silverback of our troop. He was bitten by a snake, and he lost his mind."

Prance gasped softly. "I'm so sorry. I think the sandtongues— maybe one, in particular—is using snake venom to control the other animals, make them do what it wants. I don't know why, but it wanted the hyenas gone. And before he died, Broadsight talked about shedding his skin and living again. . . ."

She broke off as she saw Bramble twitch and the baboons' eyes widen.

"There's something we need to show you," said Mud. He stood back and gestured toward Thorn's nest, and there on the ground lay a colossal snakeskin. Prance traced its coils with her eyes, her throat closing with fear.

"This is what Thorn was drawing?" she whispered. Nobody answered. They didn't need to.

After a few horrified seconds, Prance looked up to see Moonflower standing beside her. "It seems like we have a lot to tell each other," she said.

Prance watched as the Highleaves and the gorillas carefully folded and moved the snakeskin away from the Great Father's nest. It had served its ominous purpose, and nobody wanted to have to look at it, let alone step over it, any longer than they needed to.

She saw Moth sitting with Gallant on the far side of the clearing and headed over to them, her head spinning. As she got closer, she saw that Gallant was lying on his side, his back turned to the Great Father's nest. Moth looked up and gave Prance an awkward smile.

"I failed him," Gallant said. His gaze flickered up, registering Prance's approach, and then he stared at his paws again. "Great Father, and Valorcub. I failed them both."

"You didn't fail either of them," Moth said. She laid both her small baboon paws on Gallant's huge, fluffy lion paw. "You didn't!"

"I couldn't protect Valorcub," Gallant said. "I didn't know. I didn't know Menace had taken him, we all thought he was dead. And poor Valor . . ." He trailed off.

Prance wondered where Valorcub's mother was now. Was she still with Gallant's pride? She guessed that Gallant was trying to work out how to tell her that their cub was alive but had taken the name Terror and wanted nothing to do with him. She didn't know how she would have said it either.

"And I couldn't protect the Great Father," Gallant went on. "I should have been here."

This, Prance had an answer for. She knelt down in the grass beside him. "You didn't fail me. I owe you my life—that's why you weren't here. Menacepride would have killed me."

"That's right," Moth said, nodding hard. "If we'd been here to help Thorn, Prance would have died. We did the right thing, Gallant. You did. And we can't be in two places at once. Not like some," she added, looking straight at Prance.

"That's right," said Gallant. He sat up slowly and looked at Prance too. "What happened back there, Prance?"

Prance's hide prickled with self-consciousness. They were both staring at her as if they were waiting for her to explain, to make it make sense—and she couldn't.

"I don't know," she said. "I *really don't*," she added when Moth gave her a skeptical look. "It's happened twice now. It's like . . . like my shadow's gone off by itself, and I can see through it. But you can't tell anyone."

"Are you sure? Mud might be able to help," Gallant offered.

"Especially Mud," Prance said. "I mean it. Mud already doesn't trust me. I think he thinks I brought the sandtongues here. He certainly thinks this is all my fault."

"He doesn't think that!" said Moth. Then, thoughtfully, she added, "How did you know?"

"I saw you talking about it. My shadow did. Right after Thorn was bitten. I'm serious—please, don't tell him yet. I haven't been bitten, but . . . what if Mud's right, and it is dangerous, or something to do with the sandtongues? If that's true, I want to be the one to know it first. All right?"

"All right," Gallant said. "But be careful, Prance."

"And we know now," said Moth, "so no secrets from us, all right? If you think you might be turning evil, don't keep it to yourself."

Prance couldn't help chuckling at this. "I promise," she said.

Prance approached the Great Father's nest gingerly. She didn't want to disturb him, but as the afternoon wore on she'd felt more and more strongly that she needed to see him. She felt almost as if she needed to tell him her story, that if she could then it would somehow all make sense, that the way would become clear, even if he couldn't hear her or reply.

She was a few hoofsteps from the opening to the nest when she heard a voice, and realized that she wasn't the first to have that feeling.

"I know," said Mud's voice. "I know what you'd say. Everything will be all right. . . ."

His voice cracked, and Prance saw the shape of him moving through a gap in the branches. He was sitting beside Thorn, holding his hand. As she watched, he cradled it to his chest and bent his head.

She took a step back, not wanting to intrude on this moment—but something made her think she should stay within listening distance, too.

"But I can't see how," Mud said. "Not without you. You always took care of me when we were younger. I've tried to take care of you too, these last few years . . . but now I can't. I can't make it better." She heard him sniff and swallow. "The stones are telling me to find the next Great Parent, Thorn. I can't do that. You're supposed to be here! I can't do it alone, I need you. You *have* to get better, Thorn. That's an order, you hear me? Please . . ."

"*He always said I don't listen,*" said a voice. "*But I hear everything.*"

She looked down and almost swallowed her tongue as she saw the shape of an elderly baboon standing beside her. She sprang backward, her hooves skidding on the forest floor.

Thorn—a strange, translucent, shifting vision of Thorn—watched her with a faint smile. "*It's all right,*" he said.

Prance stared at him and then tilted her head to peer into the nest. She could just about make out the shape of him lying still beside Mud.

"Are you . . ."

"*Real?*" asked Thorn.

"Doing the thing I can do with my shadow?" Prance finished.

Thorn scratched his semi-visible chin. "*I think it's a little different, but you've got the right idea.*"

He walked up to her and reached up a paw to touch Prance's shoulder. To Prance's surprise, she could feel the warmth of it. It was faint, but it was there.

"*We have a journey to make together, if you're ready,*" he said.

"I . . . I think I understand," she said. She knelt down, curling her hooves underneath herself. Thorn stood back, and Prance took a deep breath and shut her eyes.

The last time she'd stepped into her shadow it had been

instinctive, accidental. But somehow, she still hadn't expected it to be *easy*. It came to her as simply as waking up from a dream—she shook off her body as if it was a thin blanket of leaves that had fallen over her in the night. She looked down and saw her hooves, shadowy and insubstantial.

"I'm ready," she said. "But . . . where are we going?"

Thorn pointed. Prance followed his finger and saw nothing but the edge of the clearing, and the forest beyond.

"To find answers," said Thorn. He put a paw on her back again. "May I?"

"Of course," Prance said and dropped to her knees to let the elderly baboon climb up. Funnily enough, though Thorn still looked every bit as old as his body, he moved like a young baboon, swinging himself up onto her back with an easy grace. She knew she wouldn't have to worry about him falling off. She could run as fast as she liked.

She started to walk and then built up speed. She passed Gallant and Moth, still talking quietly at the edge of the clearing, and wondered if Moth would see her, but she didn't hang around to find out. She darted into the forest and ran between the trees. She ran so fast she could no longer dodge as the tree trunks whistled past her, but found she didn't need to—it was almost as if the trees bent to move out of her way. She burst from the tree line onto the plains and felt Thorn's paws on her horns as he leaned between them to point at the horizon.

"There," he said, and Prance looked up to see the faint purple haze in the far distance.

"The mountain," she breathed. She didn't slow down, and she was already coming up to the river, but she still felt nervous. "It's so far," she muttered.

What if she couldn't make it? What if they were away from their bodies for too long?

She felt the steadying warmth of Thorn's paw on the side of her neck.

"Trust me," Thorn said. "And leap."

Prance leaped and yelped with surprise, and then exhilaration, as the arc of her jump took her higher. They left the plains far below and soared into the sky, Prance's hooves striking air as she ran, moving faster than any bird could fly. She looked down and saw Bravelands below. All of it, spreading out around her. There were the little forests and the endless dry plains, the glittering watering holes and the deep ravines. Then she was running over rolling hills, then steep forested slopes.

"There," Thorn said as they passed over a waterfall that crashed over the edge of a cliff into rolling mist. "The black rocks."

Prance saw them. They stuck up above the tree line, desolate and strange-looking. She slowed and began to descend, until finally her shadowy hooves struck stone, and she found herself standing on a shelf made of the black rock, beside the mouth of a dark cave. Thorn slipped down from her back and stood in front of the cave, staring into the darkness.

She turned and looked back through the trees. She could see the plains down below, hazy and bright, but the Great

Father's forest was lost in the far distance.

"I've just traveled farther than most gazelles do in their whole lives," she said. She looked down at the spirit of the Great Father. "How is this possible? Please, Thorn, why is this happening to me?"

"You have a gift," said Thorn, turning to give her a wide, fond smile. "It's a little like mine. I can travel far distances in my mind, too—not with my shadow, but borrowing the eyes of other creatures." He put a paw up and patted her neck. "I always knew you were special. I'm delighted to find out I was right."

Then his face fell a little, and he turned back to look at the cave mouth again.

"She's in there," he said. "I can sense her."

He went up to the edge of the cave mouth, and then he startled Prance by cupping his hands to his mouth and yelling into the darkness.

"Hello there! Anybody home?"

At once, Prance heard a low hissing coming from the cave. It grew louder and louder, and Thorn took a few unhurried steps back and sat down on the edge of a jutting black rock.

Sssssssssss, the hissing said, and then suddenly, when it felt like the sound was coming from the air all around her, Prance heard it shift and change into a voice. *Sssssso, you have come to my mountain.*

"I have," said Thorn to the empty air.

You waste your time by coming here, Great Father Thorn, the voice said. Prance thought she heard a note of disdain as it spoke

Thorn's name, and she frowned. *And your hours are so very, very limited, and yet you spend them on futility. The herds and flocks of your world will soon be under my control.*

"And who are you to try to control anyone?" Prance snapped.

I have many names, little shadow, said the voice. *I am the Lady of a Thousand Skins, the Mistress of the Deep Darkness. I am the voice that whispers beneath your world. The Queen of the Sandtongue.*

Something was moving inside the cave. Prance fought the urge to skitter backward, to turn and flee, as she saw that the thing had black scales bigger than Prance's hoofprints. They gleamed with a faint red iridescence. A smooth snake's head as large as a bushpig rose out of the cave mouth, towering over Thorn and Prance, as tall as Broadsight, swaying slightly as she fixed her glinting black eyes on each of them in turn. A red, forked tongue whipped from the wide mouth and tasted the air.

I have many names, said the snake. *But you may call me Grandmother.*

Prance forced herself to look up at the colossal snake, trying not to imagine how much of her was still curled in the earth beneath them. What *was* she? How could such a monstrous creature have come into being?

Your friends will become foes, Grandmother said, still swaying over them, *as one by one they heed my call.*

"Bravelands will fight you," said Thorn. "We've fought off tyrants before, and we'll do it again."

Oh yes, you will struggle, said Grandmother, *but you cannot escape my coils.* Prance shuddered as she sensed a horrible relish in the giant snake's words. Grandmother began to pull back into the darkness, and for a moment all Prance saw was the flicker of a long, red, forked tongue. *Goodbye, Great Father. I will see your friends again . . . very soon . . .*

Prance held on to her shudder for as long as she could, until she was sure the huge snake had gone, and then she shook herself. Even though her real hide was far away, her shadow-hide still crawled.

"We need to get back," she muttered. "We need to warn them. You need to call a Great Gathering, you have to tell everybody what's happening. She's wrong. She's not going to win. We won't let her."

She knelt down, expecting Thorn to swing up onto her back so she could run. But Thorn was just looking at her with a faint smile.

"Yes," he said. "You do need to warn them. I meant what I said—Bravelands knows a tyrant when it sees one. This old snake will be hard to beat, but she'll be beaten, I have no doubt about it."

"Then let's go," Prance urged him.

Thorn shook his head. "But she was right about one thing. My time. It's running out. I don't think I'm going to go home with you."

". . . What?" Prance whispered. "No, you have to! You have to come back, you're the Great Father! Bravelands needs you!"

"I wish I could. But I've had a very good, very long life, and now it's up to someone else to save Bravelands. Close your eyes, Prance Herdless."

Prance didn't want to. She had a horrible feeling that if she did, he wouldn't be there when she opened them again. But Thorn gave her an expectant smile, so she did as he said.

A moment later, she felt his paw on her shadow-side once again. It rested just over her heart.

"I'm making this part up a little bit," Thorn said softly. "It was never done for me, you see. But I think this is right. Don't be scared. You'll be wonderful."

She felt warmth on her forehead, as if he'd touched his nose to hers.

"The Great Spirit needs a new home," he said.

Prance opened her mouth to speak, but then the warmth over her heart surged and spread, filling her shadow-self with a feeling of lightness.

She opened her eyes, and for a brief moment, she didn't understand what she was seeing. Her hooves were tucked underneath her—tan and solid. She was back in her real body. And Thorn's body was here too. She was kneeling in his nest, beneath the sheltering branches.

But Thorn's body wasn't moving.

She nudged him gently with her nose, but he didn't respond.

He wasn't breathing.

Prance staggered to her hooves and rushed from the den. "Mud!" she called. "Gallant! Someone!"

Moth was the first to come skidding through the leaves, with Gallant and the two baboons right behind her. She took one look at Prance's face, and her expression crumpled.

Mud rushed up, panting and leaning on a stick, and he and Spider rushed past Prance into Thorn's nest. The Goodleaf, Grub, was with them. Prance stepped away from the entrance to the nest and watched, feeling lightheaded, as he pressed his hand to Thorn's head and his ear to his chest.

He looked up at Mud and shook his head.

"He's gone," he said with a small whimper.

Mud sat down heavily beside Thorn's body. Behind Prance, she heard a fearful hooting, and turned to see Cricket and Crab leap into the tree branches and scamper away. Dry leaves shook themselves from the branches and fell all around like rain, and a flock of bright, green-winged birds took to the sky with a cry of chirping dismay.

In the nest, Mud and Spider sat beside Thorn, both of them trembling. Spider pressed his forehead to the palm of Thorn's limp hand. Mud placed his own hand over Thorn's eyes and then cradled his head gently in his lap.

The gorillas were clutching each other's hands, and Gallant had flopped to his belly in the leaves, letting Moth bury her face in his mane.

Prance stood alone. She felt strange. Her heart was pinched with grief to see their sadness, but there was something else there now. It felt like the warm touch of a paw, protective and calming.

She would miss Thorn, but she wasn't afraid.

The Great Spirit was with her.

CHAPTER TWENTY-FOUR

Chase couldn't have imagined that life in the Sandtongue cult would
be so . . . normal.

Without an enemy to beat or a snake ritual to perform, the
gorillas mostly went about their day as if nothing had changed.
They lounged in the trees, grooming one another, gathering
food. They were acting as if the two leopards in their midst
were just oddly shaped gorillas, part of the troop.

They don't completely trust me, though, Chase thought. She kept
catching them watching her out of the corner of their eyes or
muttering to one another and glancing her way.

She guessed it was fair enough. After all, she was lying to
them.

The voice of Grandmother was quieter now than when
she'd first woken from her snakebite stupor. Chase still heard
her every so often, repeating the same mantras—the Age of

Sandtongue, the rise of Grandmother, the shedding of skin, the end of the Great Spirit. But she'd found she could tune it out.

She hadn't been asked to do anything yet, so she had simply been biding her time, watching the gorillas, trying to learn their names and their ways, looking for any piece of information that might help her later. She took another bite of the bushpig that Range had brought to her. She had felt like she didn't want to accept it at first—but she needed to keep up her cover and her strength, and she had been starving.

Range was in and out of the gorilla camp, apparently patrolling the mountain—or perhaps he just didn't like to spend too long near Burbark. She had noted with interest that their relationship was . . . complicated. Both of them were obviously used to being in charge of their own territory. If it came to a conflict, Range could talk his way out of trouble, but Burbark had a whole troop of gorillas at his back, and Range knew it.

But Range did come back frequently, and Chase soon realized it was almost entirely to spend time with her.

He really meant it, she thought as she saw him leap down from a tree and hurry over to her. *He genuinely wanted me to join him here. He's thrilled that I stayed.*

He trotted up to her, greeted her with a soft chirrup, and then lay down beside her.

"Are you feeling any stronger?" he said. "Can I get you anything else? Is it too cold up here? I know you'd normally live on the lower slopes. But when Grandmother makes her move, we'll be able to take over the rest of the mountain, and then we can live wherever you want."

Chase smiled, and it wasn't as fake as it probably should have been. "I'm *fine*. Thank you."

She looked into his eyes as he blinked happily at her.

What were you like before the curse? she wondered. His eagerness to please her was strangely sweet, or it might have been in another world. *If he's only sweet to me when I'm doing what he wants, then he's not sweet,* she reminded herself. *This isn't real. This is Grandmother's plotting.*

She couldn't help wishing that she knew the real Range, though. Perhaps he was the scheming, manipulative one, or perhaps he was the endearing, devoted leopard he was being right now. Perhaps he was neither. But it made her sad that she might never be able to free him and find out.

"I've been thinking," Range said. "About what we're going to call our first cub. Obviously, I hope we have several. But what do you think about 'Strike'?"

"I like it," Chase said, suppressing the urge to draw away in horror. *But there's no way I'll be having your cubs,* she thought.

"You two," said a low gorilla voice, and Chase looked up, quite relieved to be interrupted. It was the large Blackback called Groundnut. "Burbark wants you both."

Chase looked at Range, and she caught that flash of irritation again. He wasn't happy to be summoned. But the expression passed quickly, and he got smoothly to his paws with a charming smile.

"Are you strong enough?" he said to her.

Chase stood. She still felt a slight, genuine tremble in her paws, but she nodded. "I'm all right."

"Lead on, Groundnut," Range said, and they followed him to Burbark's nest, Range walking slowly and close alongside her so that if she stumbled, he would be there for her to lean on.

Burbark was reclining in his nest, surrounded by snake-skins. Chase tried hard not to recoil as he ran one through his leathery fingers. She felt something crunch under her paw and looked down to see an open, empty eggshell. There were several, tucked around the nest, as if Burbark himself had been laying them.

"Range," Burbark said, sitting up. "I've decided that it's time to deal with the troop who live on the eastern side of this mountain. They are small, but they are irksome to Grand-mother. Their Silverback has refused to come here and be part of the new way."

Chase took a deep, steadying breath as she heard the voice of Grandmother in her head.

We will not tolerate resistance on my mountain, she hissed. *The Sil-verback must be destroyed.*

"The Silverback must be destroyed," Chase echoed.

Burbark nodded slowly, approvingly. "We will not tolerate resistance on her mountain," he said.

She'd noticed the gorillas doing this, repeating what Grandmother had just said to them. It seemed to work almost like a secret code. They were talking to one another, but they were also simply sharing the fact that they had both heard her. She wondered how many conversations she'd had with

Range—or even with Seek—where she'd been unknowingly talking to Grandmother all along.

"Kill the whole family," Burbark added, and Chase's ears flicked back in shock before she could stop them. But it seemed like she'd got lucky—Burbark wasn't looking at her. "I would do it myself," he said, "but they know me, and they would hear me coming. Go now, as night falls. Kill the Silverback, and all of his young."

"We will do this," said Range.

"It will be an honor," Chase said, bowing her head. "To do Grandmother's bidding."

Burbark smiled and closed his eyes, running the silky snakeskin over his fingers.

The evening was chilly, and it grew more so as Chase and Range made their way along the mountainside to the east, as the sun set in the west and they moved into a portion of the mountain that was already cast in deep shadow.

The troop might be small, but with the gorilla's knowledge of where they had last been seen, they weren't hard to find. As they started to pick up the scent, Range stopped and turned to look at Chase.

"There's no need for you to endanger yourself," he said. "Burbark wants to see you prove yourself, but there's no need to take too many risks. I can sneak up on the Silverback and take care of the kill."

Chase let out a genuine sigh of relief. "I'm not up to my full strength yet," she said. "If you think you can take on the

Silverback, please, be my guest."

The idea had been preying on her mind. She didn't want to kill this gorilla. She didn't want Range to, either—if they were resisting Grandmother's influence, then these were her allies, although they didn't know it. But she could see no way that they could return to Burbark if the Silverback was alive— and no way to keep Range from coming back for her, or for Shadow or Seek, if she ran away now.

They took to the tree branches and slunk along them in almost perfect silence, until they were peering through the leaves at the small group of gorillas who sat around the roots of the tree.

Chase's heart sank. It was a *very* small troop.

The Silverback sat with his back to them, being groomed by an adult female, probably his mate. Around them, three younger gorillas were playing, rolling over in the undergrowth—a Brightback male and a younger female, with an even younger cub stumbling after them, giggling as it tried to get involved in its older siblings' game.

Chase had hated all gorillas, once. But the sight of this unsuspecting family made her heart ache.

Three of them are just cubs, and neither of the adults did anything to deserve this, she thought. *We're not hunting. This is murder.*

She couldn't stop Range from doing what he was about to do, but to kill these young gorillas would be against the Code.

I won't do it.

"They'll run," Range whispered, his muzzle pressed against the side of her face. "You go down and lie in wait for the females and the cubs."

Chase nodded and made her way back down the tree. She circled the gorilla family at a small distance until she found a place to hide. Range was right: this was the perfect place for an ambush. And it had one more thing to recommend it than Range had realized—she could position herself on the opposite side of a thick tree trunk, out of sight of the place where Range would be fighting the Silverback.

There was a thumping sound, and the peaceful mountainside suddenly echoed with howls and yowls and screams and bellows. She heard a deep gorilla voice yell, "Run!" and higher-pitched ones crying out in horror, and then the thudding of gorillas knuckling their way out of the clearing and right past her nose. She let them all pass—the younger female, the male, and the Goldback with the youngest clinging to her fur and wailing—and then she leaped from her hiding place, cornering them against a thick thornbush.

The gorilla family shrieked and cringed away from her, and the Goldback thrust her children behind her and raised her fists, ready to fight her way out if she had to. The smallest cub dropped from her back, and Chase saw all three of the others gasp as it tried to make a bid for freedom, running right past Chase. Chase put out a paw and caught the small wriggling thing, pinning it easily to the ground.

"No, please!" the Goldback cried. "Please, not my baby!"

"Listen to me," Chase hissed. "You all need to run, now. Don't wait for your Silverback. It's too late for him. If you stay on the mountain, you will all be killed. Run, and don't stop until you get to the plains."

She picked up her paw, and the gorilla cub squeaked and ran back to its mother, trembling so hard she could hardly pick it up.

"W-why are you doing this?" the Goldback stammered.

"Just *go*!" Chase growled. "While you still can."

Behind her, the sounds of fighting cut off suddenly as a gorilla's bellow turned from a full-throated cry into a rattling groan.

The Goldback stared over Chase's shoulder, her eyes wide and glistening as she listened to the death throes of her mate. Then she gave a short nod, and she and the younger gorillas turned and ran.

"May the Great Spirit go with you," Chase said.

The younger male looked back over his shoulder as he fled. "And with you," he muttered. Then they were gone.

Chase stood still, panting almost as hard as if she had fought them, until she heard Range moving toward her. Then she threw herself to the ground.

"Chase?" said Range's voice, slightly thicker than it had been before. She heard him gasp. "Chase! No!" He scrambled to her side. She sat up, taking it slowly, blinking a lot as if she couldn't focus on him. Although in fact, she could both see and smell him perfectly well. He was spattered with blood— both the gorilla's and his own. One of his eyes was swollen shut, and he was favoring one of his front paws. But he was alive, and the gorilla's blood coated the edges of his muzzle.

"Range?" she said.

"What happened?" Range asked. She saw him sniff around where the gorilla family had been.

"The Goldback got a lucky blow in," Chase said, trying to slur her words a little. "Right on the side of my head. Ugh. Dizzy."

Range looked around at the thornbushes and then looked back at Chase, and for a horrible moment, she thought, *Does he know? Can he see there was no struggle here?*

Then he shook his head.

"That stupid monkey," he snarled. "We can still catch them."

No!

"I think so . . . ," Chase said. She tried to get up, but then she let out a yowl of pain and staggered toward Range.

As she'd expected, he put his shoulder next to hers. As he propped her up, any trace of suspicion melted away, replaced with genuine-looking concern.

"All right," he said. "I've got you."

"I'm . . . still dizzy," Chase muttered. "I don't think I can go after them. . . ."

She was quite prepared to beg him not to leave her, but she stopped herself, and sure enough, Range cast a last look after the gorillas and then turned to press his forehead to hers.

"It's all right," he said. "They won't be seen around here again."

Chase leaned into him, letting him support her.

I certainly hope so.

* * *

"What will we say to Burbark?" Chase asked as they were approaching the Sandtongue troop.

"You let me do the talking," Range said. "I know how to handle that overgrown monkey. The trick with Burbark is to tell the truth, but in the right way."

Chase frowned.

"Don't worry," Range said. "We are all Grandmother's children, after all."

"Right," Chase muttered.

They found Burbark just where they'd left him. He was still awake, surrounded by a small group of other gorillas as he crouched in his nest, playing with a small snake. This time it was alive. Chase wondered if it had hatched from one of his eggs while they were away. . . .

"How did your mission go?" he asked Range, without looking up, as the leopards approached.

"A mixed success," said Range smoothly. "The Silverback is dead. Some of the others were too quick, and they got away from us."

Burbark sat up and fixed Range with a furious stare, and Chase's blood felt cold. Did Range really know what he was doing? Wouldn't it have been better to say that they'd all been killed?

He's not your friend, she told herself. *He's your captor. Let them fight, if they're going to fight.*

"And how," Burbark growled, "did that happen?"

If Range was right about telling the truth, Chase realized, she would have to say something. She opened her mouth to repeat her story about being knocked out by a lucky hit from the Goldback.

"I lost them," Range said.

Chase stared at him and then slowly looked back to Burbark.

The Silverback looked at Range for a moment, then threw his head back and laughed.

"Oh, that's good," he crowed. "Gather round, all of you! Let's hear the story of how Range, the mighty hunter, was defeated by a weak and frightened Goldback. Please, Range. Tell us."

Chase's fur prickled as she looked back at Range. He had that same look of bitterness on his face, the anger he'd felt when Burbark had summoned him in the first place—but now, it wasn't fading away.

"How dare you mock me," he snarled. His tail began to swish back and forth, and his hackles rose. "I'm not one of your pathetic lackeys who you can order to do your bidding. *I* am the one who should be giving *you* orders."

Burbark just laughed harder, and Range's eyes lit up with fury.

"I'm warning you, Burbark," he said quietly. "I've slain one Silverback today."

Range, no! Chase thought. *Don't antagonize him!*

The laughter died on Burbark's lips.

"What did you just say to me?" he snarled.

Chase took a small step back, and then another, edging as subtly as she could out of the space between Range and

Burbark. If there was going to be a fight, she wanted to be out of the way.

"I am a leopard," Range said, sniffing haughtily and raising his head so he could look down his nose at Burbark. "I obey no gorilla. It serves you right if those other gorillas escaped. Next time, do your own dirty work. I serve Grandmother, not you. I am the rightful ruler of this mountain, not you!"

Chase heard something moving in the undergrowth behind her, and she turned, her heart in her mouth, expecting to see gorillas surrounding Range.

Instead, something huge and black moved across her vision. She backed away, terrified, unable to resolve the lithe, shifting shape into something she could understand—until the head of an incredible, enormous snake lashed out from the bushes, red tongue extended, fangs as long as Chase's leg bared, and bit down hard on Range's back legs.

Range screamed. He clawed at the ground, trying to get away. Chase yowled too, horror overtaking her as Range was pulled back, writhing in terror. The gorillas watched with implacable interest as the snake began to swallow Range into its throat.

"No," he gasped. "Grandmother, please! I am a loyal servant! I was only ever loyal to you!"

The snake didn't stop.

"Please," Range begged, weaker now, his eyes rolling. They were black with pain and panic when he turned them on Chase. "Please . . ."

Chase whined and backed away, her chest hitching as she

tried to breathe. She didn't want to look, but she couldn't look away. Through the fog of horror, she kept her gaze on Range's eyes.

I'm here, Range, she thought. *Great Spirit help me—I'm here. . . .*

And then, all of a sudden, it was all over. Range's eyes rolled back, he went limp, and with a series of sickening gulps, the snake swallowed him down.

Chase fell to her belly on the ground, the forest seeming to swirl around her.

Range was gone. Eaten by his own sandtongue mistress. The leopard who'd been so kind to her when he wasn't attacking her, who'd stolen her cub and then let it go again, who'd only wanted to share his awful, twisted life with her. If he hadn't lied to cover for her . . .

One by one, she became aware that the gorillas had fallen to their knees or their bellies too, prostrating themselves in front of Grandmother. She looked up. The snake was so impossibly huge that her coils wound around the trees. She reared up, raising her head easily to the level of the lower branches, so that she could look down on her troop. Chase realized that she could see Range, a slight lump in the massive throat of Grandmother, and she felt sick.

Only the strongest and most loyal will march beside me, said the voice in Chase's head. *Range was proud. He became weak, and so he sacrificed himself.*

I wouldn't call that a self-sacrifice, Chase thought. She felt as if she was on the edge of true hysterics, but she dug her claws into the ground and tried to hold on.

Only those who are dedicated first to the cause are worthy to be my family, Grandmother hissed. *The time is upon us, my children. The Great Father is dead.*

No! For a horrible moment, with her head spinning and her heart feeling strangely broken, Chase almost thought she had said it aloud. But she couldn't have, or she would have joined Range in Grandmother's jaws.

The gorillas hooted and bellowed and thumped their chests in triumph, and Chase took a deep breath.

She couldn't let her guard down now. Range had bought her a chance. She had to take it.

She let out a yowl that she hoped sounded pleased, not simply terrified.

Nothing will stop us now, said Grandmother. *Soon, my children. Blood will flood the plains!*

"Blood will flood the plains!"

"Nothing will stop us! Blood will flood the plains!"

All around her the gorillas began to repeat the phrase, and Chase took a deep breath and forced herself to join in.

The wild, cacophonous sound seemed to take root in her chest, and soon it didn't matter what the words were. Surrounded by enemies, standing in front of the Lady of a Thousand Skins, Chase born of Prowl turned her face to the stars, and she screamed.

EPILOGUE

Windrider banked in the air, feeling the currents buffeting her ancient wings. The chill made her old bones ache. Her thinning feathers could hardly lift her from the ground these days. Her own time was almost upon her, but she thought she still had a year or two in her yet, especially if she could keep finding comfortable columns of air to drift upon.

She had seen Bravelands thrive under Great Father Thorn, and she had seen the troubles begin again, as they had so many times before. Now she circled over the Great Father's clearing in the forest, observing the chaos below without much concern. The grasstongues, and the smaller, less steady of the birds—they were always so upset when a Great Parent died. But she had seen several of them come and go in her long, long life, and she would live to see the next one take Thorn's place.

Already, she felt a stirring in the wind. The Great Spirit

was on the move. It lived on, after the bodies of the hosts were dust, and so Windrider was satisfied.

Stormrider came swooping up beside Windrider, flapping in that youthful way of hers rather than sitting atop the currents like a sensible vulture.

"Windrider, something's wrong," she squawked.

"I know," said Windrider.

"Not the Great Parent," said Stormrider. "Something else. It's the deaths, Windrider. They taste wrong. Not all of them, but *lots* of them. Something is spreading through Bravelands. Something bad."

"I know," Windrider said again. "And we must be vigilant."

She looked down at the animals who swarmed the plains, many of them converging on the last Great Father's resting place. Baboons, giraffes, elephants, rhinos, and many more, she knew, who Stormrider would be able to see with her sharp, youthful eyes.

"The Great Spirit is moving. It will find its next host," she said.

"When?" Stormrider asked.

Windrider chuckled to herself. "Not for us to say, young one. We are vultures. We wait, and watch. Perhaps the Spirit has chosen already, or perhaps the next Great Parent has no idea what awaits them. These are dangerous times, after all." Windrider turned her beak and blinked calmly at her great-great-grand-chick, as she turned her aching wings to whirl away across the plains. "When the Spirit calls to us, we will be ready."